SAILORS AND SIRENS

THE J.R. FINN SAILING MYSTERY SERIES

C.L.R. DOUGHERTY

SAILORS AND SIRENS

The J.R. Finn Sailing Mystery Series

Book 4

Vigilante Justice in Florida and the Caribbean

"That is the Island of the Sirens. Circe warned me to steer clear of it, for the Sirens are beautiful but deadly.

They sit beside the ocean, combing their long golden hair and singing to passing sailors. But anyone who hears their song is bewitched by its sweetness, and they are drawn to that island like iron to a magnet. And their ship smashes upon rocks as sharp as spears."

From Samuel Butler's translation of Homer's Odyssey, Book XII

1

THE TARGET'S BEDROOM WASN'T AS DARK AS THE GROUNDS OUTSIDE his mansion. I could see outlines of the furniture through the sliding screen door from the patio. The night was pleasant; the sliding door was open. Only the screen kept me outside.

His perimeter security was good, but I dealt with that already; my client briefed me on it. The two guards were sleeping peacefully with the help of my tranquilizer darts. They would awaken in about an hour, no worse for wear and with no memory of having been unconscious. Besides the guards I immobilized on my way in, there was still a two-man security team inside the house. They were off duty. According to our intelligence, they stayed in their quarters until they were due to relieve the two outside. As long as I was quiet, they wouldn't be a problem.

I reached into the pouch at my waist and retrieved a handkerchief soaked with silicone lubricant. Wiping it along the tracks at the top and the bottom of the sliding doorframe lessened the chance of noise when I opened the screen.

I grasped the handle of the sliding screen and pushed gently, testing. The frame moved smoothly, without a sound.

Stepping into the target's bedroom, I stayed to the side of the opening, partly in the shadow of the drapes. Once inside, I could tell the dim light in the room came from a nightlight in the adjoining bathroom.

When my eyes grew accustomed to the shadowy light, I saw the woman. She wasn't supposed to be here, but there she was, sleeping alongside the target. I stood, watching the two of them sleep while I considered my options.

I could abort the mission and let him live another day or two. Or I could consider the woman collateral damage. My client wouldn't care as long as I didn't leave her body behind, but I wasn't comfortable with killing the woman. Killing her and removing her body without awakening the sleeping guards would be tough. I didn't like either of my options.

The injection I planned for the target would induce cardiac arrest, and it would leave no trace. He would die within a minute or two after I administered the drug, but he would be in agony for that brief period. Chances of the woman sleeping through his death throes were slim, and she might arouse the sleeping guards. I would have to kill her first to avoid that, but that might awaken the target. Then he might awaken the guards.

Either way, killing both of them meant I might have to kill the two inside guards. I wouldn't have time to dispose of three bodies. Then there would be questions about the target's death, which wasn't acceptable.

I was on the verge of deciding to abort the mission when the woman woke up.

Sitting up on the edge of the bed, she cradled her face in her hands; her elbows rested on her knees. I wondered if she was hung over; that's the way she looked. She ran her hands through her hair for a few seconds.

I held my breath when she got to her feet. She took a step in my direction, but then she turned. Shuffling into the bathroom, she closed the door. I saw the bathroom light come on under the bottom edge of the door as a vent fan started.

Moving quickly, I rounded the foot of the bed. The woman turned down the sheets when she got up, and the target was lying on his back without a stitch of clothing.

I stuck the needle into his femoral artery and pushed the plunger. He was stirring as I pulled the syringe away and dashed back outside. When I paused to close the screen, I heard him begin thrashing and screaming.

The woman would hear him, too, but that was okay. She wouldn't know what happened. An autopsy would find that his death was from natural causes, which was according to plan.

I ran across the yard to the security fence. When I climbed the fence on my way in, I dropped a grappling hook and its line inside the fence. I found them with no trouble, and I was over the fence within 30 seconds after administering the lethal injection.

As I walked to my rental car, I took my phone from my pocket and called my client.

"Yeah?"

I recognized the voice; Aaron Sanchez was an Army buddy from years ago.

"Is Elena there?" I asked.

"You got the wrong number. No Elena here."

"Sorry to disturb you," I said. "Have a nice night."

"Thanks," Aaron said, disconnecting the call.

The prearranged exchange told Phorcys my mission was a success. Aaron and I started using Elena Howard's name for coded messages when we were at Fort Benning together 20 years earlier. She wasn't a real person — just an imaginary barfly we used to tell stories about in the barracks.

Ten minutes after my call to Aaron, I was in my rental car, driving a little under the speed limit as I negotiated the 30-minute trip to my hotel. I resisted the urge to hurry; I was expecting to find Mary, my lady friend and fellow assassin, waiting when I got there.

TRAFFIC WAS light heading into Miami at 3 a.m. Driving was easy. I passed the time thinking about how I came to be here and why I just killed a member of the President's cabinet at his Florida hideaway.

Not long ago, Mary and I joined an organization that was formed by a few retired senior military officers who were disenchanted with the corruption at high levels in our government. Patriots to the core, they took their oath to uphold the constitution seriously. Principled and accustomed to putting their ideas into action, they decided to help the still-functional parts of our government sort out the mess.

Before that, I was working for a small, secret group within the U.S. Department of Defense. I discovered that my boss of 20 years and several other high-level government officials were running a game of their own on the taxpayers' tab and using me to do their dirty jobs.

Mary and I met as I was leaving Puerto Rico on one of my last missions for the DoD. At the time, I thought our meeting was by chance. She presented herself as a seagoing hitchhiker, a footloose young woman looking for adventure. As I got to know her, there were things about Mary that made me nervous, but that's a story for another time.

After a few days, I knew that there was a lot more to Mary than I thought when we met. She was on the run from the mob for one thing. And for another, she was a killer for hire. Three thugs caught her alone on my boat in Bequia and tried to kidnap her. Without batting an eye, she killed one of her assailants and escaped.

Later, when we were in a bind and needed reinforcements, she made a phone call. Identifying herself as Medusa, she asked to speak to Phorcys. Phorcys worked magic on our behalf. Mary told me that Phorcys was an occasional client of hers, and one who owed her favors.

Back then, Mary and I both thought Phorcys was a pseudonym for a person. Later, when Phorcys recruited me, we discovered that it was the name of an organization. When Phorcys approached me about joining them, I found out that several members were people I knew and trusted.

I was invited to become part of Phorcys by a man named Mike Killington — Lieutenant General Michael Killington, U.S. Army, Retired. Affectionately known to his troops as "Killer Mike," he founded the covert group within the Department of Defense that was my employer until recently.

Mike was responsible for my joining that DoD operation all those years ago, although he moved on before I transferred into the group. I knew him only by reputation until about ten days ago. Now he was my boss, or as he put it, I was one of his partners. But I knew better. He was my boss, no matter what he said.

Another member was also a retired general with whom I was acquainted. Bob Lawson was running that secret operation within the DoD when Aaron and I joined it as junior officers.

My old friend Aaron Sanchez was one of them, too. He became part of Phorcys shortly before I did. Aaron and I went through basic training and Officer Candidate School together over 20 years ago. From there, we both joined that secret group in the DoD. He was the intelligence officer I worked with for most of my career as an operative in the field.

Mike Killington and Bob Lawson knew me from the old days. They realized that I was about to become the unwitting instrument of corrupt bureaucrats, my former boss among them, so they sent Mary to look after me, but I only learned that later.

Given our similar skills, it wasn't a surprise that Mary and I formed a bond beyond that of ordinary coworkers. We wrapped up our separate assignments and were ready for a break when Phorcys came clean with us. Thinking we had some free time, we were contemplating an extended cruise on my sailboat, *Island Girl*. Then we got drafted into Phorcys. Only ten days ago, that was. It seemed longer. Things were happening quickly.

Phorcys gave us a list of targets; Mary left Tortola for Florida six days ago. She was supposed to do preliminary reconnaissance. I stayed behind in Tortola to get the boat ready for long-term storage. We didn't know when we might get to begin that cruise, but I hoped we would meet up this evening in my room.

I was a little worried as I took the exit for my hotel. My last contact with Mary was when she landed in Miami six days ago. I got a brief note from her in the blind email drop we used, telling me she arrived safely and would be in touch later.

Before she left Tortola, we agreed to meet tonight at the nondescript place where I was staying. I hoped her long silence didn't mean trouble, but in our line of work, you never knew what might happen.

Back when Mary and I set up tonight's rendezvous, I didn't yet know about the mission I just completed. It was assigned to me this morning as soon as I arrived. A lot could have happened with Mary in the last few days, too. Maybe she was waiting for me, and maybe she wasn't.

Flipping the blinker on, I turned into the parking lot of the seedy hotel that billed itself as "a part of Old Florida." I checked in earlier this afternoon and scoped out the room, but I left my duffle bag in the car in case my plans changed. For all I knew, after I carried out my first mission, I might be on the run. Killing the Secretary of Defense wasn't exactly a low-profile hit, but I got away clean.

Hoping to see a light on in the window of my room, I was disappointed. I left a key with the desk clerk for Mary, but the window was dark. Maybe she was asleep; it was almost 4 a.m.

Retrieving my duffle bag from the trunk, I locked the rental car, pocketing the keys as I fumbled for the room key. I climbed the stairs to the second floor and unlocked the door, stepping into the vestibule. Dropping my bag, I closed the door behind me.

I entered the room, feeling for the light switch. Blinded by the bright ceiling light, I blinked and found myself staring down the muzzle of a Colt Model 1911-A1. Forty-five caliber was not quite a half-inch, but it looked big enough for me to fall into.

"Hello, Finn," the man holding it said.

2

BEFORE I REACTED, HE LOWERED THE MUZZLE AND LAID THE PISTOL on the bed where he was sitting. He extended his hand. "I wasn't sure who was coming through that door," he said.

"Pointing a pistol at me is a good way to get yourself killed," I said as I shook his hand.

"I know. I figured it was worth the risk, given the situation. You really think you could have taken me?"

"No doubt in my mind. The time you took to say 'Hello, Finn' gave away your advantage. I could have taken the pistol by the time you finished."

"Why didn't you, then?"

"I recognized you, Aaron. Lucky for you. Once I start moving, there's no pause button. It's muscle memory."

"You still look the same, Finn; just a little weather-beaten. And I have recent pictures of you. But I've changed a lot, and you haven't seen me in almost 20 years. How did you recognize me so quickly?"

"Two things: your voice and the scar."

"Okay, I can believe the voice part; we spoke on the phone half an hour ago. But I don't even notice the scar in the mirror anymore; I had plastic surgery to get rid of it. It's there; I can find it if I look for it, but..."

"When that guy cut your throat, I was there, Aaron. The plastic surgeon did an okay job, but I knew where to look, once I heard the voice. Why are you here?"

"We have a problem with the woman."

"She was in the bathroom the whole time," I said. "She couldn't have seen me. As far as she knows, he had a heart attack, like we planned."

"What are you talking about, Finn?"

"The woman in bed with Sanders when I got there; I was trying to decide whether to waste her or abort the mission when she got up and went in the bathroom."

"There was a woman there with him? Is that what you're saying?" Aaron frowned. "His wife was supposed to be in Washington."

"Yeah, I didn't figure her for his wife. She was too young and hot. At least if your taste runs to strippers."

Aaron laughed at that. "I bet his Secret Service detail is going nuts trying to figure out how to spin that one. Or somebody up the line is."

I waited until his chuckles died down. "What woman were you talking about, then?"

"Mary," Aaron said. "Or whatever name she's using at the moment."

"What about her?"

"She's off the reservation. You got any idea where she is?"

"No," I said, feeling my brow scrunch up. "Last I heard from her was when she landed here six days ago."

"What did she say then?"

"That she was on the ground and in a hurry. She would be in touch later. But I haven't heard from her."

"You left a key for her downstairs, Finn."

"I did?"

"Don't bullshit me, man. Why are you doing that?"

"Getting even for the pistol in my face."

"I told you I wasn't sure who was coming through that door."

"You thought it would be Mary? Were you going to shoot her, or what?"

"I knew it wasn't her. We paid the desk clerk to take a break; I've got somebody on the desk. He would have called me if Mary picked up the key, okay?"

That made sense. It was what I would have done, in Aaron's position. "Yeah, okay."

"So, tell me, Finn. Why did you leave a key for her?"

"Before she left Tortola, we set up a rendezvous here for tonight."

"How did you pick the time and place?"

"She picked it. It was a week after she left. I already knew I would be in Miami. She said she used this place before."

"But neither of you could have known what Mike would ask you to do between then and now."

"No, but we have backup plans, Mary and I. Not our first time around the block, remember?"

"Where's your next rendezvous spot then? And when?"

"Not so fast, Aaron. I've been open with you so far. Show me the same courtesy. What's going on here? You and Mike are the ones who sent her into my life. I didn't just pick her up and spring her on you. Now give."

"That's fair enough, but I'm not sure what to tell you. We didn't even know she arrived in Miami safely. No check-in, nothing. We've left her messages, but she's not responding."

"Uh-huh," I said. "I don't know what to say, Aaron. Any chance somebody knew she was coming?"

"You mean besides me and Mike?"

"Yeah. Anybody else?"

"No," Aaron said. "I mean, Bob Lawson probably knew; Mike would have told him. You thinking we might have a leak?"

"Hey, it happens to the best of us, sometimes."

"No. No way. Neither of us told anybody, or even mentioned her where we could have been overheard. I'm sure Bob didn't give her away. How did she make her travel arrangements?"

"We didn't discuss it, but she's done this before," I said. "You know how good she is. My guess is she did it the way she usually does. Either she pays cash at the ticket counter or uses a prepaid credit card she bought with cash. I don't know what name she used. She was Mary Louise Brannon when we cleared into the BVI last time. But that doesn't mean much."

"It's something," Aaron said. "Do you know where she got that passport?"

"No. She used it when she flew from Miami to Puerto Rico to meet me, and it was fresh then. So she kept using it. Mary has passports stashed all up and down the East Coast. She built most of those identities herself. I only got the one passport for her, through Nora's operation. But you know about that. Did you or Mike help her with any of those identities?"

"No. She declined our help. She's a control freak."

"Yeah," I said. "She and I share that. It's what keeps us field agents alive."

"Do you know for sure she was in Miami when she sent you that last message?"

I thought about that for a couple of seconds. "No, I guess I don't."

"Do you still have the message?" Aaron asked.

"No. You thinking maybe you could trace the origin? Even for our blind web mail account?"

"Probably not. Unless it was actually sent. You still leave 'em in the drafts folder, like we were doing?"

"That's right. But I deleted that one after I read it. That's the way it works, remember?"

"Yeah, sure," Aaron said. "Unless she hit the send key, there's no way to trace a draft email like that. So we don't know for sure where she went when she left you in the BVI, and we don't know what identity she's using. The damn woman's invisible when she wants to be."

"And that's why Phorcys uses her," I said. "You knew that about her at the beginning. Don't bitch about it now."

"Yeah, I know. It's a feature, not a bug. But it can still be a pain in the ass."

"There's no reason to think she didn't fly to Miami."

"But she stood you up," Aaron said.

"Yeah, maybe. Could just as easily have been the other way around."

"I guess we don't have any choice but to wait and see if she shows up at your second rendezvous, huh?"

"Right. Or she may get a message to me. But..."

"But what, Finn?"

"Given her past and the number of people who might be after her, this might not be her doing." I didn't like harboring that thought, much less sharing it, but things like that happen in our business.

"Yeah, somebody could have snatched her. That occurred to me. She's been damned reliable. This is out of character. Can you think of anyone who might have taken her?"

I shook my head. "No. But I have an idea for you."

"What's that, Finn?"

"You started out with her working through her agent, or broker, or whatever she called the woman."

"That's right. So?" Aaron asked.

"So you know who that woman is. Maybe you could question her?"

"Slow down, boy. First, we don't know who she is. We know how to get in touch with her, but she makes Mary look like a publicity hound. She's so invisible she might not even be a real person."

"You serious?" I asked.

"What do you mean, am I serious?"

"About her not being a real person. You think she's a chimera? A fabrication?"

"It's crossed our minds," Aaron said.

"Our?" I asked.

"Mine and Mike's. She could even be a creation of Mary's, you know."

"That reminds me," I said. "A few times, Mary hinted at having access to unusual resources — people she could call on for specialized stuff. Once I found out you and Mike sent her to me, I thought maybe it was through you two."

"Well, yeah. We've backed her up from time to time, but I know what you mean. We ran into that with her. Mike and I figured it was through the broker. You know Mike was her contact, not me, right?"

"Yes. Maybe you should ask him about that."

"No need; we discussed it in depth before we decided to bring her on full-time. We don't have a clue. Is something bugging you, Finn? Something she said, maybe?"

I shrugged. "I don't know. Nothing specific, but early on, I wondered if she worked for somebody — I mean, besides contract clients. Some government agency, like."

"Our government? Or another one?"

"Good question. But after I found out about the Dailey and O'Hanlon hits my suspicion faded. Once I got my head around that, I figured her for a top-notch contract killer. That's what she claimed to be."

"Her performance supports her claim," Aaron said. "We need to move on, Finn."

"Move on? What are you saying?"

"Whatever comes out of this Mary business, we need to put you to work. We can't wait on her. Too much shit's happening. Don't take offense, but I have to ask you something before we get into that."

"Okay. Ask," I said.

"Can you keep your head in the game with Mary missing? Or is that going to distract you?"

I laughed. "You aren't serious, are you?"

"Dead serious. I need to hear you say it."

"You know what I am, Aaron. It's like I'm two different people. One's a boat bum, and the other is the one you've known about since Fort Benning. You with me?"

"Yes, so far. But what about Mary? Where does she fit?"

"She's the same way. The part of her that's a regular 24-year-old girl, that part of her is in love with the boat bum. And vice versa. The other person who's part of Mary, well, it suits that person to work with the Finn that you and Mike know. You get what I'm saying?"

"Yes, but — "

"I'm not finished, Aaron. Think of it like Mary and I each have a dark side, okay?"

"Okay."

"Our dark sides are separate from the normal sides. The Finn that you know would kill Mary in a heartbeat if she threatened him. And the dark side of Mary? Well, she'd blow me away without batting an eye, if she needed to. You understand?"

"Yeah. That's bizarre, man. Heavy shit. A shrink would have a field day with you, but as long as you believe what you just told me, that's what matters."

I locked eyes with Aaron. "I believe it."

"Yeah, I can see you do."

"Do you believe it, Aaron?"

"Yeah. You aren't the first one who's told me something like that."

"Mike?" I asked.

"No comment."

I smiled and nodded. "Tell me about all this work you have for me."

3

SITTING ON THE RIM OF A PLANTER AT THE INTERSECTION OF
Jefferson Avenue and the Lincoln Road Mall in South Beach, I
sipped my *café colado*. I watched the crowds of people ebb and
flow. It was around 10 p.m.; the tourists still outnumbered the
oddballs. I kept an eye on the people coming and going from the
Pink Parrot, a trendy nightclub. There were two husky bouncers
outside the door to keep the tourists out.

"You have to be somebody to get in the Parrot," Aaron told me
earlier.

I spent most of the day with Aaron at Mike Killington's house
in Coconut Grove. I met with Mike for a short introduction, but
my day was filled with briefings from several of Aaron's staffers.
Before the show started, Aaron cautioned me that I was to stay
anonymous as far as the staff was concerned.

The briefings covered the extent of the corruption in our
government. A good amount of what I heard was for background.
Mike and his friends intended to clean up as much as they could
by selective exposure and anonymous tips to the news media.
They planned for Mary and me to handle the worst of the worst.

The intent of the briefing was to give me some perspective on the long list of targets. Mike and his friends in Phorcys wanted me to understand that not every politician or bureaucrat was on the list. Without some background, it would have been easy for me to think we were carrying out a wholesale purge.

After my briefings, I spent several hours in my hotel room catching up on the sleep I missed last night. This evening, I was scouting for my next target, who was known to frequent the Pink Parrot. Or "The Parrot," as Aaron told me it was called by the in-crowd. My goal tonight was preliminary reconnaissance. The target was a drug lord, although he was known publicly as one of those people who are famous for no particular reason except that they're famous.

Kyle Brandon, his name was, and he was making noise about leveraging his fame into a run for a seat in the House of Representatives. That wasn't going to happen.

The pictures from my briefing showed Brandon to be a handsome man in his early thirties. He was described as a hard target, which amused me. After hearing about Brandon, Aaron and I took a break of a few minutes before the next session.

"Wipe the smirk off your face," Aaron said, when we were alone. "What's so funny?"

"The notion that a bogus celebrity is a hard target just tickled my funny bone after the hit last night. That's all. When they went on about his lack of security, it was all I could do to keep a straight face."

"Yeah, well, don't get cocky. Brandon's not the kind of person you've dealt with. It's not a security detail that makes him a hard target. It's the environment. He's shrewd — never goes out in public alone. The only times he's ever exposed, he's surrounded with innocent hangers-on. The potential for collateral damage is high. That would be a disaster."

And that's why I was sitting here on my perch watching the crowds. I wanted to see for myself what the potential for collateral damage might be. My musing was interrupted when I saw a stretch Hummer pull to the curb on Jefferson Avenue, a few yards from the stop sign at Lincoln Road.

It was about 50 feet from me when three of the doors popped open. Three bulky men in loose-fitting, brightly patterned shirts jumped out. They closed the doors behind them and scanned their surroundings. In the glare of the street lamps, I could make out the clear plastic tubes running from the backs of their necks to their right ears. Those were the type of radios that top-notch security people used. Their shirts hung outside their belts, and the telltale bulges over their right hips told me they were armed. A fourth man stayed behind the wheel, his eyes in constant motion as he watched the crowd.

After about thirty seconds, one man took up a position on the corner opposite me, the corner closest to the Parrot. A second man walked up to the doorman and spoke a few words. The doorman nodded and grinned. The bodyguard's lips were moving, though he faced away from the doorman, looking back at the Hummer. I figured he was on his radio, giving the all-clear to the people inside the Hummer. The third man was standing near the Hummer. He nodded and moved his lips. Turning, he opened the left rear door of the big, ugly vehicle.

Expecting Brandon to step out, I was surprised to see the first passenger alight. He was a small man with unattractive features, dressed in an expensive, custom-made suit with a white shirt and tie. At 11:00 on a sultry Miami evening, he stood out from the crowd. He turned to the interior of the Hummer and barked a command, but I was too far away to make out what he said.

Two attractive but overdone young blonde women climbed out, their spike heels giving them trouble as they stepped from the running board to the pavement. The overdressed man leaned into the vehicle and gestured impatiently, then stepped back to make way for a third girl.

With flowing auburn hair, she was by far the most attractive of the three. She gave him a haughty look before planting her left foot on the running board. As she held that position for a couple of beats, her slit skirt fell away to expose her left thigh. Her hand grasped the fabric, closing the gap, but not before I saw the tattoo. Even from 50 feet away, I recognized it. I've been admiring it at close range for quite a while now.

As I was recovering from my shock, she reached the pavement. I stared at her face, squinting. It was Mary, all right, but I'm not sure I would have recognized her except for the cobra tattoo. She wore heavy makeup like the other girls, and her hair was... well, it was just wrong. Mary wasn't looking in my direction. Her attention was on the little man in the suit, who offered her his arm. I watched as he escorted her and the other two girls into the Parrot.

Shifting my attention to the Hummer for a moment, I made note of the license plate number. I wanted to know who she was hanging out with. I sent an encrypted text with the plate number to Aaron asking him to run the registration. Meanwhile, I got to my feet and ambled over to the Parrot's entrance.

The doorman stepped into my path when I was about two paces from the door. He glared at me and shook his head, holding up a big hand in a stop gesture. I took a 100-dollar bill from my pocket and offered it to him. Smiling, he shook his head again.

"Wish I could, man, but it's a private party. Sorry."

I nodded and walked away, losing myself in the crowd. The doorman was watching me; I was finished for the night. Walking west on Lincoln Road, I came to the garage where I left my rental car.

Twenty minutes later, I was back in my hotel room. The message light on my room phone was flashing. I picked up the phone and followed the instructions on the card beside it to retrieve my voicemail.

"I told you not to try to talk to me again, asshole," Mary's voice said. There was loud music and the sound of shouted conversation in the background. She made the call from the Parrot, given the background racket and the timing.

"That trick with you and your pal Mike was a onetime deal," she said. "You knew that going in. What is it you don't understand about *onetime deal*? I did what you kinky bastards wanted; you paid me. The end. And it cost me every damn penny you paid me to get square with Louie after you blew it tonight. His security guys saw you watching me outside the club. Keep it up and they'll make both of you sorry. Nobody messes with Louie's girls like that and lives. Now get — "

"Enough, bitch. Gimme that phone," a man's voice said, interrupting her. He disconnected the call, leaving me to wonder what she'd gotten herself into.

I examined the instruction card for the voicemail, but I couldn't find a way to retrieve the calling number. I would leave the recording intact for now and talk with the front desk in the morning. Maybe they knew of a way to pick up the caller ID. Aaron might be able to help, if I asked, but something told me not to. Not yet, anyway.

It was midnight. I wouldn't hear from Aaron about the plate number until sometime tomorrow morning. Asking him to expedite the license check would invite him to ask for an explanation. So would asking him to find out about the origin of the voicemail. I didn't want to tell him about seeing Mary just yet — not until I found out what her game was.

As for the voicemail, it told me Mary herself spotted me. Her line about Louie's security men seeing me was bullshit. Whoever Louie was, his goons wouldn't have noticed me. At most, they saw me try to enter the club. Still, I was one of several people turned away by the doorman between the time Louie and his girls went in and the time I tried my luck. So it was Mary who saw me. She didn't miss much.

She left the voicemail, but why? Was she trying to send me a message? That was the only explanation that made sense. If she were trying to lose me, she wouldn't have made the call. I worried over her words like a stray dog with a fresh bone, but I couldn't find any hidden meaning.

She mentioned the name Louie, and as good as told me he was a pimp, but I could see that, anyway. A high-class one, maybe, but a pimp all the same. Mary would know that I would have somebody run the license plate; that was the kind of thing people in our business did. I would end up with the name of the Hummer's owner. Would it be Louie? And if so, what would that mean?

Mary also mentioned Mike. Maybe she wanted to be sure I passed this along to him, whatever *this* was. Or maybe she wanted to be sure I didn't pass it along. Yawning, I shook my head, fighting to stay awake. I gave up and climbed into the bed. As I was dropping off to sleep, it came to me that Mary borrowed the phone to make the call. Was it Louie's phone? Or somebody else's? And why did she do that? Was there hidden meaning there, or did she just not have a phone of her own?

I sat up on the edge of the bed while I organized my thoughts. I could wrestle with them tomorrow. Once I was sure they were committed to memory, I lay back down and surrendered to sleep.

4

Fresh from a hot shower, I was shaving when my phone pinged. *Probably a text from Aaron with the license plate information.* I leaned around the bathroom door, peering at the clock on the nightstand. It was 9:30. Sleeping late was a rare thing for me, but I was tired from several days of irregular rest. Morning wasn't prime time for surveillance of Kyle Brandon, so I slept in.

He would be easy to find during the workday, but my first choice wasn't to kill him during normal working hours. Too many people would be around, given that he was spending his time at his campaign headquarters. I would prefer to catch him during the evening, when he was arriving or departing from his residence. My thought was that he would have fewer people around him then.

Finished shaving, I stowed my gear and went into the bedroom. I picked up my phone and entered the unlock code. My guess was correct; there was a text from Aaron's number. I opened the encrypted text app Phorcys used and read his message.

The Humvee belongs to Louis M. Rayburn. Got a Miami Beach address, but he won't be there. Call me after you check the local news.

I lifted the remote from the nightstand, but then I thought better of turning on the TV. Hungry, I decided instead to eat breakfast at the diner across the street. I ate dinner there last night.

The place was a throwback to the days of serious greasy spoon joints. They had an early vintage color TV that made everybody look like a victim of a nuclear blast. Tuned to a local "all news, all the time" station, it hung on the wall and drowned out the continuous, shouted arguments between the cook and his wife. She served as the waitress and cashier.

The diner was empty when I walked in. I took a stool near where the waitress stood behind the counter. Her mouth hung open as she watched the TV with the oddly tinted people on the screen. After grumbling something at me that could have been "Good morning," she poured me a cup of coffee. Then she stood there, glaring at me with her stubby pencil poised over her pad, annoyed that I was disturbing her.

"Two eggs over easy with grits and sausage," I said.

She licked her pencil and scribbled on the pad. Looking up at me, she asked, "Toastergravybiscuit?"

"Biscuits and gravy, please."

"Jews?"

"What?"

"Jews. Awrange er termater. Which one?"

"Orange juice, please." I suppressed a chuckle. It wouldn't be funny to piss her off. No telling what she might say or do.

"Uh-huh." She scribbled again and tore the order off her pad like she was angry with it. She waddled over to the pass-through window to the kitchen and hung the order on a wire, screaming something unintelligible through the opening.

She planted her massive rear end on a wooden barstool near the pass-through, careful not to break the stool, and turned her attention back to the local news. I swiveled to the side, facing the strange old TV, and listened to the newswoman. She was interviewing a hard-looking older woman in front of a run-down South Beach condo building.

"You knew him, then? Mr. Rayburn, that is."

"Louie? Oh, yeah. Everybody knew Louie. Piece-a-trash, that's what he was. Always bringin' hookers up to his place. This ain't that kinda buildin'. We got people with kids livin' here. It's a family place. We been tryin' to get him outta the buildin', but I guess we ain't gotta worry 'bout that no more."

"He brought hookers here, you say?"

"Uh-huh. Couldn't miss knowin' what them women were up to. Trash, they were. Not just one, either. Two, three at a time. Sometimes more. My husband and me, we figgered him for a pimp. Looked like it, acted like it. And them women." She pursed her lips and shook her head.

"Mrs. Wells, you said you live on the same floor as Mr. Rayburn?"

"That's right. One door down, across the hall. We got a sea-view unit. Cost way more, but it's worth it. 'Specially now we ain't gonna have that scum across the hall. We been praying to the Lord for help ever since he moved here. Guess our prayer's been answered, finally. The Lord works in mysterious ways." Mrs. Wells shook her head.

"Were you at home when the police came this morning?"

"Honey, we sure were. I seen the whole thing. Couldn't-a missed it, anyhow. Louie and them three thugs of his, they made an awful racket. Yellin' and screamin' like you wouldn't believe. Then it got real quiet-like. Me and Harlan figgered they drunk themselves into a stupor, that's what. Harlan, he knew some men what drank like that when he was in the service, you know."

"Is Harlan your husband?"

"Of course he is. I wouldn't let no strange man in my place. I ain't one o' them harlots like Louie brought around. Trash. That's what. Harlan's upstairs, talkin' to the police detectives. They done already talked to me; said I could go. They wanted to hear Harlan's version of things."

"So there were three men with Mr. Rayburn?"

"Yep. The same three that was always with him. Big, rough-looking boys, with them radio things in their ears like the secret service. And Harlan says they carried guns. Harlan knows about stuff like that, from bein' in the service. He said them boys was bodyguards."

"Did Mr. Rayburn always have armed bodyguards?"

"He sure did. Didn't do him much good, though. That sleazy girl killed all three of them big men, plus Louie. O' course, Louie was just a little feller, but mean lookin' just the same."

"Tell me about the girl, Mrs. Wells."

"One of them hookers, she was. Had on real high heels and a dress slit up to...well, you know. Them three bodyguard fellers drug her into Louie's place."

"You say they dragged her in?"

"Well, they didn't quite drag her, but there was one of 'em holdin' each arm and one right up close behind her, like. Louie was walkin' in front, so they had her boxed in where she couldn't get away."

"Was she trying to escape, Mrs. Wells?"

"She couldn't, the way they was all around her, holdin' onto her. But I sure woulda been, if it was me in her place. Not that I'd ever get myself in a fix like that. Stupid whore. Me and Harlan figgered she was gonna get what she deserved. Asking for it, them hookers are, the way they dress and paint themselves up."

"Do you think she was the killer?"

"Couldn't a been nobody else. She was the only one there besides Louie and them boys."

"How can you be sure, Mrs. Wells?"

"The elevator. It's right next to our bedroom. Can't nobody come or go that we don't hear it."

"What about the stairs?"

"Right next to the elevator shaft. We hear the door open and close. Elevator or stairs, don't matter. Either one wakes us up."

"So you didn't hear anybody after Mr. Rayburn and his bodyguards dragged the girl into his unit, is that right?"

"Yep. That's it. Nobody came or went after that. And the screamin', it started not long after they got here. Didn't last too long, neither."

"How do you suppose the girl got out?"

"What?"

"Did you hear the girl leave?"

Mrs. Wells frowned for several seconds. "Why, no. Now you mention it, we didn't. Wonder how she snuck out? Or maybe she's still there."

"You told me you saw them removing corpses, Mrs. Wells. Is that right?"

"Yep. Four of 'em. Cops said it was Louie and three men. Didn't say nothin' about the girl. You think she's still in there?"

"I don't know, Mrs. Wells. It's time for a commercial break." The frowsy blond with the heavy makeup looked into the camera. "Heather Newcomer, Channel 5 News, live from the scene of the latest grisly murder in South Beach. Mrs. Wells and I will be back in five minutes. Stay tuned for all news, all the time."

When the commercials started, the waitress hoisted her bulk from the stool and retrieved my breakfast from under the warming lights in the pass-through. She put the plates in front of me: one with two cool, rubbery eggs; another with two biscuits slathered with glistening, greasy sausage gravy.

"Awrange jews coming right up," she said, turning back to the pass-through.

She was settled on the creaking wooden stool again in time for the return of Heather Newcomer. I ate as much of the breakfast as I could stomach. It would have been better before it got cold, but I understood. I was transfixed by the news myself. When I finished, I held up three five-dollar bills, fanned out. When the waitress saw them and nodded, I put them under my coffee cup and left.

I needed to walk around the block and think about things before I called Aaron. He was sure to have questions. Hell, I wondered what was going on myself. But Aaron didn't know about Mary's involvement, and I wasn't sure I should tell him.

DESPITE WHAT I said to Aaron earlier about my relationship with Mary, I did feel personal loyalty toward her. I wasn't lying about the dark side of my psyche, nor about Mary's, but this wasn't a matter where our ruthlessness came into play. Whatever Mary was doing, I didn't see how it could be at threat to me or to Phorcys, so I would protect her privacy.

Aaron said she was off the reservation. She started working with Phorcys before I did, so I wasn't sure about her arrangement with them. She didn't offer them exclusivity, from what she told me. After a while, though, they booked all her available time, so she was effectively only working for them. That might not preclude her serving other clients if she chose to do so.

Now that I thought about it, my relationship with them was similar. Until Mary came along, I never knew Phorcys existed. When Mary took up with me, I was retired from the Department of Defense. I was doing occasional contract work for them, still taking orders from my former boss, Phyllis Greer. At least, that was one of the names she used. Then I discovered Phyllis was a traitor, and further, that she sold me out personally. That was when Mary and I killed her.

Mary and I planned to kill Phyllis's boss, too. He was part of whatever scheme she was involved in. Before we got to him, he fell victim to a Russian mobster. Aaron was still trying to identify the Russian.

The man I killed the night before last was the next one up the chain of command. Phyllis's boss was a Deputy Secretary of Defense. My target the other night was the Secretary of Defense himself. That's why I was so careful to make it appear that he died of natural causes. The Secretary was dirty, but he didn't know the details of the operation Phyllis ran. After the Russian mobster's people killed Phyllis's boss, there was no one at the DoD to assign targets to me.

That made me a free agent until I connected with Phorcys. I wasn't looking for assignments from anywhere else. But as I reflected on my "welcome aboard" meeting with Mike, he made it clear I was a partner in the organization, as opposed to being an employee.

There was no mention of any prohibition on my taking on work from outside. I guess Mary's situation was the same, but I still wondered who else she was working for, and why. Whoever it was, they were important enough to Mary for her to stand me up, not to mention failing to stay in touch with Phorcys.

Earlier in my relationship with her, Mary mentioned unfinished business that predated her involvement with Phorcys. Maybe that's what she was doing now, but why would she have cut herself off from me, or from Phorcys? That was unlike her. As Aaron said, she was dependable.

I struggled to think of other possibilities, situations that would explain her behavior. When I saw her get out of the Hummer last night, she didn't appear to be under duress. But neither did the other two girls, presumably hookers from Louie's stable, and I didn't think they were free to come and go at will. Pimps didn't work that way. And there were the three bodyguards.

Mrs. Wells, Louie Rayburn's neighbor who was on the TV news, described a woman who could have been Mary being forced into Louie's condo. Then there was a lot of screaming, followed by silence. I wondered when the police were called, and who called them.

If the Wells woman called them, she would have no doubt mentioned it during her interview. I could have missed that part, though. Given her comments about the screaming and noise, she or her husband probably made the call. Besides, she would have jumped at the chance to lodge a complaint. She made her dislike for Rayburn clear enough.

According to her, the noise started almost as soon as Rayburn and company were inside his place. My guess was it got quiet when Mary finished off her would-be captors. Or it was possible she killed the three bodyguards and then interrogated Rayburn. That could explain the screaming. Mary would have left using the stairs, most likely, and she wouldn't have let the door to the stairwell give her away.

I was sure Mary killed Rayburn and his goons, but I couldn't fathom why. Was it a hit for another client? That didn't seem likely. She wouldn't have put someone else ahead of Phorcys — unless there was a personal angle to this. Even so, it was unlike Mary not to let me or Phorcys know she was going to miss her scheduled contacts with us. Something about this didn't make sense.

I couldn't delay my call to Aaron much longer. Opting to get it over with, I found a bench at a bus stop and sat down. I took my new, Phorcys-supplied iPhone from my pocket. It looked identical to my other one, but Aaron's tech support person assured me it was not. She explained that this one was running a custom operating system developed by someone she knew. The software provided for advanced encryption, as well as feeding randomly modified identity information to cell sites. That meant the phone couldn't be tapped, nor could its location be tracked.

5

"AARON?"

"Yeah. That you, Finn?"

"Yes. You wanted me to call."

"I did, yes. Have you seen the morning news yet?"

"You mean about the guy who owned the Hummer?" I asked.

"Yeah. Talk to me. What's going on?"

"I was watching for Brandon at the Pink Parrot. The Hummer pulled up and a guy who looked like a pimp got out with three bodyguards and three women."

"So?" Aaron asked. "Was Brandon with them, or what?"

"He wasn't with them, but I wondered if Rayburn was meeting him. Brandon didn't enter the club while I was watching, but he could have been inside already. Rayburn and his bunch created a big stir when they entered, so I sent you the text. Then I tried to get in, but I didn't make the doorman's cut. I tried to bribe him, but he turned me down. He said there was a private party, but who knows?"

"Did you keep up the surveillance? See who left when the club closed?"

"No. The doorman was watching me after I tried to get in. I didn't want to attract any more attention, so I left."

"Yeah, okay," Aaron said. "That was probably smart. There's more to that place than meets the eye. We've got somebody working inside the club, anyway. I'll see what I can find out and let you know, but why would you think Brandon was meeting with a pimp?"

"I said the guy in the Hummer looked like a pimp. I'm not sure he was one, though."

"Why's that?" Aaron asked.

"With all that security, he didn't look like your ordinary pimp. And he was dressed like a banker or something. I want to know who he is; his pimp act wasn't all that convincing."

"Security? You mean the three guys who were found with him?"

"Yes," I said.

"Just hired muscle, I imagine. You have a different idea?"

"Yes, I do. They were pros, Aaron. Damn good at what they were doing. They weren't the kind of yardbirds I would expect to see with a pimp."

"What are you getting at, Finn?"

"The pimp thing could be a cover."

"A cover? What do you think he was, then?"

"I don't know, Aaron. Do you know any more about him?"

"Only what's in the news," Aaron said. "I'll do some checking, but I can't push too hard, given what happened to him. If we ask too many questions about him, we'll attract attention from the cops in a hurry."

"I can see that," I said. "Anything could be helpful, though."

"Yeah. I'm on it. What's your next move on Brandon?"

"I'll watch for him to leave his campaign headquarters this evening. I want to see how he travels — what kind of entourage he has. I'm worried about collateral damage."

"I hear you. Any word from Mary?"

"No. You heard anything?" I asked.

"No. What do you think about that? Worried?"

"No, but it's like I said the other day. I have a job to do. I can't let Mary distract me. Have you talked to Mike?" I asked.

"Mike? About what?"

"Mary," I said. "She seems to have a one-on-one deal with him."

"Yeah, that's true. I've noticed the same thing. But he hasn't heard from her. He knows she missed her check-ins. He would have said something if he'd heard from her. Any plans for the day besides staking out Brandon's headquarters?"

"I just finished breakfast. I'll walk it off and head back to my room. Sack out for a while. I'm trying to get myself adjusted to working the night shift, you know?"

"Yeah, man," Aaron said. "Keep in touch, and call me right away if you hear from Mary."

"I will. You do the same. And let me know about Rayburn, please."

"Will do," Aaron said. "Sleep tight."

He disconnected the call and I put the phone in my pocket. I sat there for a few minutes, thinking. Then I did what I told Aaron I was planning to do.

BACK IN MY room after a walk around the neighborhood, I checked the email drop that Mary and I used. I didn't expect to find anything there, but I checked it every morning and evening. That was part of our routine. Mary surprised me this morning — and not for the first time. She was dependable, but that wasn't the same as being predictable. She left me a message in the drafts folder. I opened it, noticing that she sent it while I was out for breakfast.

Hi, Sailor!

Sorry about the crazy voicemail last night, but I needed to wave you off, and I couldn't get any privacy. I hoped you would read enough between the lines to at least guess at my message and keep your distance.

I owe you an apology for disappearing, too, but something personal has come up. I need to finish it while I can. It's important to me, and no one can help me with it — not even you.

You know by now that I missed my check-in with Phorcys when I got to Miami. I've smoothed that over, but only a special contact there knows what's happening. Don't worry; I'm not burning any bridges with them. I should be back to work with you and them soon.

About us — I know you're not the jealous type, but I want to tell you shouldn't read anything into what you saw last night. Those four jerks are dead now; it wasn't what it looked like.

One last thing. I know how tight you are with Aaron, but he's not in the loop on this, so please don't mention any of it to him. I hope you haven't already told him about last night, but if so, just play dumb from here on. I'm sorry to put you in a bind with him, but if he asks about me, sandbag him as best you can. It's not that I don't trust him. It's just that it could embarrass the person I talked with at Phorcys.

I have to run; I'm short of time, so I don't know when I'll be in touch again. Don't worry. This is nothing I can't handle, and I'm in a big hurry to get back together with you.

Love,

Mary

So much for my plans to crash and sleep through the day. My mind was awhirl with the possibilities. Mary said this was personal. That meant it must be part of something she was involved in before she began working with Phorcys.

There were large gaps in what I knew about Mary's background. Piecing together things she told me, I figured out she was killing for hire while she was still in college. She mentioned beginning her working relationship with the woman she referred to as her agent or broker back then. But we didn't discuss how she got to that point, or how she survived her teens.

Mary was on her own from the time she was 12, but I suspected that she didn't have a normal childhood even before that. Her mother was a hard-core drug abuser, and that conjured up nightmare images of what Mary must have endured before her mother died. That she managed to get through her teenage years and finish college at a normal age spoke to her determination and resourcefulness.

Until now, she avoided giving me details of that period in her life. She once remarked that she knew I would imagine the worst. "But I would rather leave it to your imagination, Finn. Whatever you think I might have been doing then can't be as bad as the reality. I have to live with the things I did, but I can't bring myself to talk about them. Not even with you."

To give that some context, Mary wasn't easily embarrassed. In our short time together, I saw her do things that made even my battle-hardened stomach churn. I took her at her word when she said she could handle what she was into now. But I was still bothered by her showing up at the Pink Parrot while I was watching for Kyle Brandon, my current target. Like most people in my line of work, I'm suspicious of coincidence.

Miami's a big place. There are plenty of trendy clubs that appeal to people like Brandon. The Pink Parrot was one of them, from what Aaron told me.

The Parrot didn't look like the kind of place that would cater to pimps and hookers. Rayburn's bodyguards looked like they should have been wearing expensive suits and protecting a senior government official. And the doorman recognized them. *Rayburn was no ordinary pimp, that's for damn sure.*

I resigned myself to wait until I heard from Aaron about Rayburn. No amount of speculation on my part would produce answers I could depend upon. Plus, it would be nice to know if Rayburn met Brandon at the Parrot. I couldn't articulate a reason why I suspected that. *Put it down to intuition and move on, Finn. You'll know soon.*

Whatever happened inside the Parrot, Rayburn took Mary home with him. Mrs. Wells, the woman on the TV news, didn't mention any other women last night. And she made it sound like Rayburn and his security didn't give Mary a choice about joining them.

I thought about sending Mary an answer, but I was tired, and in four hours, I would have to leave to set up my surveillance at Brandon's campaign headquarters. I would have plenty of time to think about what to tell her while I watched for him to leave.

I pulled the drapes closed and took off my shoes and trousers. Stretching out on the bed, I willed myself to sleep.

6

SLOUCHED BEHIND THE WHEEL OF MY RENTAL CAR, I KEPT AN EYE ON the storefront office that was Kyle Brandon's campaign headquarters. It was a little after four p.m. My guess was they would close up shop around five. I was parked on the opposite side of the street, and in a place that allowed a view of most of the office through the plate-glass window. It looked like a typical campaign operation.

There were six people working, most of their time spent on telephone calls. Occasionally, one of them would get up and walk back into a corner that was out of my field of vision. After a few minutes, the person would return to the desk area and pick up the phone. I was betting Brandon's private office was back in that corner.

Sure enough, at about five p.m., Brandon emerged from the corner and stopped in the middle of the open area. He propped one hip on the conference table that occupied the center of the space and chatted with the troops for a few minutes. When he went back to his office, the workers began packing up to go home. Soon, there was only one person, a young woman, left. She went back to the corner and came back with Brandon. He walked her to the door, saw her out, and locked the door behind her.

As he walked back to his office, he paused by one of the now-empty desks and picked up a telephone. Since he held it to his ear and began talking without touching the base of the phone, I knew he answered an incoming call. He nodded a few times, his lips moving, and then returned the receiver to its cradle. He half-leaned, half-sat on the desk, looking out the window. One foot on the floor, the other swinging back and forth, he grinned and shook his head.

I was beginning to wonder about him when I glimpsed movement in the rearview mirror. Shifting my eyes, I saw a woman approaching from behind. She was on my side of the street, but when she reached the corner, she crossed and walked along the sidewalk toward the entrance to Brandon's campaign head-quarters.

Attractive in a no-nonsense way, she had dark hair, arranged in a bun on the back of her head. In the fading light, I couldn't get a good look at her face. Carrying a briefcase, she wore a dark blue business suit with a white blouse and sensible, low-heeled black shoes. *A lawyer or accountant? Some kind of consultant?*

When she passed into Brandon's view, he stood and walked to the door, opening it as she approached. She went inside, and they shook hands. *An after-hours business meeting.*

Brandon locked the door behind her and turned to the big, storefront window. He fiddled with something for a second and lowered the Venetian blinds. The blinds were open, and I saw the woman put her briefcase on the nearest desk and open it. She took something out and turned to face him. As he began closing the blinds, I saw that she was holding up a filmy, short négligée. Then the blinds blocked my view.

In a few seconds, the lights in the front office went off. There was dim light still showing around the edges of the blinds. The lights in Brandon's personal office must still be on. *So much for the after-hours business meeting.*

I wondered who the woman was. Not Brandon's wife, for sure. His wife was a stunning, six-foot-tall blonde in her early twenties. The woman with the briefcase wasn't even in the same league. *Stolen watermelons always taste better, though, as an old buddy of mine used to say.*

Settling in to wait, I revised the tentative plan I came up with after I saw the staff leave. Until his visitor showed up, I thought maybe Brandon worked late. Slipping into the office while he was there alone would have been a perfect setup — no collateral damage, plenty of privacy to do what I needed to do.

Given the lack of traffic in the area, I could steal a few computers to make his death look like a burglary gone wrong. When Aaron and I first discussed the hit, I was thinking I would make it look like a drug-related killing. An interrupted burglary would raise fewer questions, though.

The people in the front office all worked on laptop computers, and I saw several of them put the machines in their desk drawers before they left. I could just stack the laptops in a cardboard box ready to carry and leave them there after I dispatched Brandon. The cops would figure the burglar panicked after killing Brandon and left without his loot.

My thoughts were interrupted by the flash of headlights in my car's side mirror. It wasn't yet dark, but the light was fading. I watched the car pull out and come my way. Just as it drew even with me, another car turned onto the street from a side street. It was headed in the opposite direction, and its headlights illuminated the driver of the first car as it passed me.

It was the brunette in the business suit, but her hair was mussed now. Her attention on the oncoming car, she didn't notice me watching her as she drove past. *How did she slip by me? She didn't come out the front door. A back door? Did she take the alley up to the cross street? But why?*

Once the two cars were gone, I got out of my rental and locked it. Walking up to the corner, I planned to check on that back door. I might even go inside, depending on what I found. My target was still there, unless he slipped out the back as well. If he stayed in the office, he would be alone. I could cross one more off the list, with any luck.

THE ALLEY behind Brandon's campaign headquarters was much darker than the street. There were only a couple of security lights, and the narrow alley was in the shadow of the buildings. There were a few waste bins pushed up against the walls, leaving just enough room for one vehicle to pass. Turning into the alley, I walked in the shadow of the wall that would be the back wall of the office. Brandon's place was the third one from my corner. Counting the doors as I passed, I found his with no trouble.

There was a button beside the door with a card that indicated I should ring for admittance. There were no visible security cameras; I checked before I entered the alley. Just in case, I wore a baseball cap pulled down over my face. There were dreadlocks attached to the cap. As long as I didn't look straight up into a camera, I was well disguised.

Studying the door for a moment, I saw that there was a keyed deadbolt above a normal, locking doorknob. The position of the hinges told me the door swung into the building. I slipped on a pair of nitrile gloves and put a hand on the doorknob, turning it slowly. When I felt the latch disengage, I pushed gently, testing to see if the deadbolt was in use. The door moved, swinging in slightly. I put more pressure on it, hoping the hinges wouldn't squeak. I was in luck.

I stepped into a dark space and closed the door behind me. Feeling my way as my eyes adjusted to the pitch black, I saw dim light outlining another door which must open into the office space. I crept toward the light, my arms extended, shuffling my feet to avoid tripping over anything. When I reached the door, I took a deep breath and turned the knob, pulling the door toward me.

Stepping out of the storage area, I found myself in the main office. The only light now came from outside, leaking around the edges of the blinds over the big plate-glass window. The place was deserted. I turned toward the corner where I thought Brandon's private office was. The outline of a closed door was just visible in the dim light. *Did Brandon leave with the woman? She was only here a minute or two — were they that quick? Or did they decide to get a room somewhere?*

I opened the door into Brandon's office and took my smartphone from my pocket. Closing the door behind me, I switched on the phone's light and flashed it around the office. When I saw Brandon sitting in a swivel chair behind his desk, I flinched. His arms were secured to the arms of the chair with cable ties, and the front of his shirt was soaked with blood from the gash that opened his throat. His tongue protruded from the cut — a Colombian necktie, a strong sign that the killing was drug-related.

I turned off the light on my phone and retraced my steps to the alley. Staying in shadow, I removed my gloves and shoved them into my pocket as I made my way up to the cross street. There was no traffic, so I took off my baseball cap with its attached dreadlocks and stuffed it in my shirt front. I walked at a normal pace to my rental car, unlocked it, got in, and drove away.

7

DRIVING BACK TO MY HOTEL, I WAS CAUGHT IN THE TAIL END OF
rush hour traffic. That gave me plenty of time to mull over what
happened to Brandon. The woman killed him; there wasn't any
doubt about that.

There wasn't enough time between her departure and my
arrival for anyone else to have done it. Based on the short time
she was in the campaign headquarters, she worked fast, too. My
estimate was that she spent five minutes with him, no more. She
was efficient.

In that short time, she managed to persuade him to let her
cable-tie him to the chair. Given the négligée she took from her
briefcase, I could guess how she talked him into that. Female
assassins aren't unheard of in the drug world, but they're still
rare. It's a macho business. Rare though they might be, one just
killed Kyle Brandon. Her technique pointed to the involvement of
a cartel.

It crossed my mind that she took my target, not that it bothered me. She wouldn't be happy to know I saw her, though. I
wasn't about to tell the cops, but I was obligated to let Phorcys
know that someone else beat me to Brandon. Did one of his

competitors in the drug trade put out a contract on him? That's what it looked like, but then I considered setting up his death so that drug traffickers would be blamed, myself. Maybe the woman did the same.

Speaking of the woman, the coincidence factor wasn't lost on me. Last night, I saw Mary disguised as a hooker, and four people died — one who might or might not have been a pimp. Was the woman I saw tonight Mary? I honestly couldn't say.

I wouldn't have recognized her last night except for the flash of thigh that gave me a glimpse of her cobra tattoo. The nondescript businesswoman who called on Brandon could have been Mary in disguise.

I didn't know much about how she handled her work. I only saw her kill twice, and neither time required a disguise. She killed two other times while we were working together, but I wasn't present for either of those.

Last night's hooker disguise was flawless except for that slit skirt. Tonight, there was nothing about the woman who killed Brandon that made me think of Mary. On reflection, the woman I mistook for a lawyer was about Mary's height, but she looked heavier, and the hair was wrong. A wig and some padding? Could be, I guess. Women were good at altering their appearance; there were whole industries devoted to helping them. Odds are it was Mary.

That was two kills for her — that I knew of — since she missed her check-in with Phorcys a few days ago. Based on the message she left for me earlier today, these hits were personal.

She didn't say how long it might be before she came back to me, but from the tone of her message, she didn't think it would be long. Or maybe that was wishful thinking on my part.

I still didn't know if her two victims were connected, but given that she killed them both in quick succession, I suspected they were. Her choice of the Colombian necktie for Brandon intrigued me, too. Why did she pick that?

She didn't have the benefit of the briefing on him that I got from Phorcys. She must have pegged him for a drug dealer somehow, or she wouldn't have killed him that way.

I was turning into the parking lot at my hotel. It was time to think about what to do next. Aaron owed me the information on Rayburn; he would probably have something by now. He wouldn't bother me until I called him; he knew I planned to spend this evening watching Brandon.

Still, I should call him tonight. Brandon's body would be found in the morning when his campaign staffers showed up for work. His death would be all over the morning news.

Speaking of coincidence, I didn't want Aaron or the other people at Phorcys to start wondering about me. Last night, I asked for a license plate check that turned up Rayburn. This morning, he was dead. Tonight, I was watching Brandon, and in the morning, his body would be discovered.

I needed to get ahead of the game, for a change. I still didn't want to tell them about Mary, no matter how strong my suspicions were. But I would definitely leave her a message in our blind email drop. If I were going to cover for her, I needed a little more background.

BACK IN MY ROOM, I got a cold beer from the minibar and sat down in the easy chair in the corner, my feet on an ottoman. I took a sip of my beer and called Aaron.

"What's up, Finn?"

"I have news on Brandon, but first, tell me what you've learned about Rayburn. Was there a connection between him and Brandon?"

"Sometimes I wonder if you're psychic," Aaron said. "Yeah, there was a connection. I'll start at the beginning, though, okay?"

"Sure. Whatever you think. I'm listening."

"Okay. Rayburn wasn't a pimp. He was a political consultant."

"There's a difference?" I asked.

"It may be a fine line, in this case," Aaron said, with a chuckle. "But we'll get to that in a minute. Let's talk about the murders at his condo first. You said you saw the news reports?"

"Some of them, yes," I said.

"Did you catch any of the interviews with his neighbor lady?"

"Mrs. Wells?" I asked.

"That's the one. My source got access to the Miami Police Department's murder book, okay? So what I'm giving you is what really happened, as best the cops can piece it together."

"All right. Give it to me. Why are you hedging?"

Aaron normally cut to the chase, without going into detail on his sources.

"Because the cops think the Wells woman is full of shit. They've got no sign anyone was in Rayburn's condo that night except the four victims. The place was cleaned by Rayburn's maid service the day of the killings. It was pristine as far as any trace evidence, except from Rayburn and his bodyguards. You with me?"

"Yes. Go ahead," I said, thinking *Way to go, Mary!*

"You were right about the bodyguards. They were pros, all right. Retired from the U.S. Marshals Service, all three. Now, here's how the cops think it went down. One of the three body-guards lost it. He shot the other two and kneecapped Rayburn. That accounts for the screaming the neighbors heard."

"Mrs. Wells mentioned that, but no gunshots," I said.

"Yeah. Several other neighbors heard the screams — and no shots. The killer used the victims' bodies to suppress the sound of the shots. Contact shots in the belly and up through the chest, except for the last one. I'll get to that."

"That's wild," I said. "I'm surprised the neighbors didn't hear something."

"Yeah, well, don't forget all the screaming. Probably missed the muffled shots in the confusion. The killer really jammed the muzzle into the victims to make a good seal. Nasty entry wounds."

"What about the kneecapping?" I asked.

"Two shots were muffled with a throw pillow. And at some point, he held the pillow over Rayburn's mouth."

"You mean like to suffocate him?" I asked.

"The cops don't think so. They figure it was to stop his screaming. The killer tied Rayburn to a kitchen chair with his hands cuffed behind him, probably after he killed the other two bodyguards. Then he used a heavy pair of those compound action, locking pliers to crush ten of Rayburn's knuckles."

"An interrogation?"

"Could be, but the cops think it was sadistic, maybe some kind of screwy revenge. After the killer got tired of messing with Rayburn, he shot him in the back of the head and then killed himself. Single shot under the chin. Muzzle buried in soft flesh again; same pattern. Took the top of his own head off. That argues against interrogation as the motive for the torture. No chance for him to use any info he might have gotten."

"No, I guess not," I said, thinking. *But it might make sense if Mary were the killer. Maybe she needed info on Brandon.* "You said there was a connection between Rayburn and Brandon?"

"Yeah. Rayburn was advising Brandon on his campaign."

"Aha," I said.

"'Aha' is right, but there's more," Aaron said. "Now I'm going to change sources — this didn't come from the cops. I'm guessing they're satisfied to close the Rayburn case without more investigation. I mean, why not?"

"They've got a nice, self-contained murder/suicide," I said. "Why make extra work?"

"Right. I told you we have a source at the Pink Parrot, remember?"

"Yes."

"Okay. This is why I said you were psychic. You saw Rayburn

and his party go in the Parrot. Seems that Brandon was already there. He was at a table with two young guys who just started working on his campaign. Rayburn's security detail stayed back in the shadows and covered him.

"Rayburn took the three girls up to Brandon's table and the four of them sat down. Two blondes and one with auburn hair. They had a few drinks. Pretty soon, the two young guys had the blondes sitting on their laps. The third girl, the auburn-haired one, sat there between Rayburn and Brandon while they shot the breeze. It was a welcome-aboard party for the two new staffers.

"After an hour, Rayburn and Brandon shook hands, and Rayburn and the extra girl left. Our source saw Brandon slip her a business card before she stood up. He scribbled something on it before he gave it to her. Then Brandon made arrangements to cover whatever his two staffers spent, and he left them with the blondes. That foursome closed the place down in the wee hours and left in a cab. And that's about it."

"That's quite a bit, Aaron."

"Yeah. Not sure what it means. Now, you said you had news on Brandon."

"You'll hear about it on the news in the morning, once his staffers show up for work," I said.

"You nailed him already?"

"Not me. Somebody beat me to it. I watched from a car parked across the street as his campaign headquarters closed for the day. Brandon locked the door behind the last staffer to leave. Then he went back toward where I figured his office was. I gave him around 30 minutes, and then I tried the back door. I thought Brandon was by himself, or that he slipped out the back way."

"And what did you find?" Aaron asked.

"The back door opens on a narrow alley, and it was unlocked. I let myself in and felt my way through the dark into the main office. His private office was back in the corner where I thought it was, but there was no light coming under the door. I figured it was empty, so I decided to have a look." I told Aaron how I found Brandon.

"I'll be damned," Aaron said. "But how did that happen?"

"I couldn't see the alley from my car. Somebody could have approached the back entrance from any number of places. They could have left the same way. The irony is that I ruled out trying to make it look drug-related — figured that might get more attention than we wanted. I planned to make it look like a burglary gone wrong if I caught him in there alone — an interrupted burglary."

Aaron laughed. "I guess he must have crossed the wrong person. The Colombian necktie says it all. Be interesting to see where this one ends up. Sorry we wasted your time, Finn."

"No sweat. And thanks for gathering the background on Rayburn. It wasn't for nothing; at least I know I was right about Rayburn and Brandon. And the retired marshals still bother me. How about you?"

"I just collect the information. It's you operational types who process it," Aaron said. "What about it bothers you?"

"I don't know yet. Put it down to intuition for now, but something will bubble to the surface, eventually. I'll let you know. Why would retired U.S. Marshals work for somebody like Rayburn? And three of them? There are too many pieces that don't fit — like Rayburn procuring girls for Brandon to reward his troops with. He was a pimp, after all. I called that one right for whatever reason. Maybe just because we already knew Brandon was dirty. But he was on your list, and Rayburn wasn't. Something's still not right, there. My gut says Rayburn might have been connected to other targets."

"He could've been, I guess. You know where we got the list, though."

I knew about that list. Mary was working for Phorcys when she stole it from some high-level mobsters who aren't with us any longer. She was trying to escape the repercussions when she hitched a ride out of Puerto Rico on my boat a while back, but that's another story. Several other stories, actually.

"Yeah, I know where it came from," I said. I chuckled for a second, remembering.

"Why do you ask, Finn? About him being connected to other targets, I mean."

"I'm thinking about the targets yet to come."

"I'm not following you," Aaron said.

"We already know Brandon was connected to several of the future targets, right?"

"Yeah," Aaron said. "So?"

"If Rayburn was connected to some of the same ones as Brandon, they might be getting nervous. One of their dirty friends getting whacked could be written off as the kind of shit that just happens, but two in two days?"

"I see what you mean. You want me to check on Rayburn's contacts?"

"If you can, it's probably worthwhile. We don't really know how comprehensive that list is — just that the people on it were taking bribes. There could be layers that the keepers of the list didn't know about — people like Rayburn, who were connected to the people taking bribes."

"Good point," Aaron said. "I'll do a little checking. If you don't have a problem with it, I'll run that by Mike and Bob, too. They might not have thought of expanding on the list."

"Sounds like the right thing to do," I said.

"On a different subject," Aaron said. "With Brandon down, are you moving on to the next one?"

"Yes. I thought that was the plan. Why?"

"It's the plan. You need to know he left yesterday, planning to spend ten days at his place in the Bahamas."

"Thanks. Lyford Cay, or Eleuthera?" The next target had two Bahamian getaways.

"We think Eleuthera, but we're still checking. He stopped off at his place in Lyford Cay, but we think that was just to pick up his boat. I'll let you know. Anything else we should talk about?"

"Not that I can think of. I'll be in touch as my plans take shape."

"Okay, then. Good talking with you; stay out of trouble."

"Yeah, I will. You too. Bye for now."

I disconnected the call and took a big swallow of my beer. I needed to work my way through all the new information before I responded to Mary's message.

8

AFTER WHAT AARON TOLD ME, I WAS SURE THAT MARY KILLED Brandon as well as Rayburn. I was awestruck by the effectiveness of her disguises, too. Except for my brief, accidental glimpse of her tattooed thigh as she got out of Rayburn's Hummer, I wouldn't have recognized her. That was a talent of hers that I didn't know about.

Mary left the Pink Parrot with Rayburn after he hooked the other girls up with Brandon's staffers. The Wells woman described the girl Rayburn and his minions hustled into his condo as wearing a skirt "slit up to... well, you know." Coupled with the timing, that left little doubt that the girl was Mary.

Mrs. Wells gave the impression that Mary might not have been a willing guest. Knowing Mary, though, she let them push her around until she got them where she wanted them. I was sure her intent was to get them all inside Rayburn's condo where she could kill them without witnesses. Rayburn's intent was a different question. What did he have in mind when he coerced her into joining him in his condo?

That left me wondering about her interrogation of Rayburn.

What did she need from him? Or did he just piss her off and pay the price? Only Mary could answer those questions.

Aaron's source said that Brandon had given the girl in the slit skirt a business card with something written on the back. That was no doubt a note related to the assignation I witnessed this evening. Rayburn must have introduced Mary and Brandon, but why? Was Rayburn indeed nothing more than a pimp masquerading as a political consultant?

The answers to those questions might have some bearing on the project Phorcys assigned to Mary and me. Whatever the answers might be, they weren't likely to address my biggest question, though. What was Mary up to? It was personal, she said. Did that mean she and Rayburn knew one another? Did she have more "personal" hits planned?

My head was spinning. I drained the last swallow of beer from the can and took it over to the wastebasket. There was another beer in the minibar. I decided I might as well drink it. I was too wound up to sleep.

With Brandon out of the way and my next target *en route* to Eleuthera for a week, I wasn't in any rush. I retrieved the second beer and took it back to the easy chair. As I took my first sip, I considered whether to send a message to Mary before I planned my next hit.

I missed her. The last woman I was so attached to was my ex-wife, and we parted company almost before Mary was born. I wanted to be part of Mary's life, and for her to be part of mine. That feeling was mutual, but we both had other things going on in our lives right now. Until the last few days, I thought we were focused on the project that Phorcys assigned us. Phorcys and I both thought Mary and I were part of their team. Now I wondered if Mary found her personal agenda more compelling than our shared goals.

Her personal agenda... I shook my head and took another sip of beer. Trying to figure out her personal agenda was a waste of time. I was sure she would tell me all about it, but not until it was a *fait accompli*. I wanted to write her, but I couldn't think of anything worthwhile to say.

She missed our rendezvous here the other night, and I would miss our next one, still two days away. I would be in the Bahamas, probably in an anchorage off Eleuthera, on a boat I was yet to acquire. I wouldn't put that in a message to her. What was the point?

Putting Mary out of my mind, I began to think about my next target. John F. Hawkins, known to television audiences throughout the southeast as Honest John. Hawkins started a franchise operation that sold used cars.

The franchisees pooled their inventories, so their customers could shop at one location and choose from cars in the pooled inventory. For a small fee, a customer could put a hold on the vehicle of their choice and have it brought to their local franchise for an inspection and test drive. If they purchased the car, the fee was refunded.

Hawkins implemented some clever ideas, like selling at a "no haggle" price and using professional-looking showrooms. He offered a thirty-day, no-questions-buy-back guarantee, too. Those things weren't unique, but he implemented them well and helped the franchisees operate efficiently.

That was one of the things that put Hawkins in my sights, that efficiency. He offered his franchisees two main advantages over his competitors. One was low-cost financing of their inventories. Hawkins was laundering drug money, making low-interest loans to the franchisees. The other advantage was in labor costs. There were a lot of semi-skilled jobs in the used-car business, and Hawkins provided his franchisees with illegal immigrants who had false work permits.

Those were the things that put him on the lists that Mary stole from a mobster named O'Hanlon. Hawkins was one of many participants in a conspiracy organized by O'Hanlon. An evil genius, O'Hanlon knew that a lot of criminal enterprises shared the same needs. Many of those needs could be satisfied by funneling money to corrupt government officials. O'Hanlon's scope had been broad; he had an extensive network of government officials on his payroll.

Once Mary stole O'Hanlon's lists for them, Phorcys developed a two-pronged strategy to return the government to the people. One thrust was to expose corrupt officials and leave the authorities no choice but to prosecute them. The other was to eliminate the crooks the government wouldn't prosecute.

That's where Mary and I came in. Some of our targets were government insiders. Others, like Hawkins, were private citizens who were beyond the reach of the government.

Hawkins's illegal activities had made him one of the country's wealthiest men. Like many other rich people, he thought he was a law unto himself. Given the extent of the O'Hanlon-fueled conspiracy, Hawkins wasn't wrong about his impunity. But that was about to change.

Tomorrow, I would find a boat to buy. It's easy enough to fly to Eleuthera from Miami, but once there, I would need a place to stay. Even traveling under an alias, I would leave a trail that the authorities could follow. Besides, Eleuthera isn't a big place. It's a long, narrow island, with a population of around 10,000. The people are spread out; anywhere I stayed, I would be noticed, and getting to Hawkins's private compound at Savannah Sound might attract attention.

Eleuthera was a couple of hundred miles from Miami. I could leave Miami and sail 40 miles to Bimini, where I could clear into the Bahamas with all the other local boaters from the Miami area. Arrivals like that were so common that the customs agents were pretty relaxed about it. You filled out their forms and paid your fee and that was it. Then you could go anywhere in the Bahamas without further ado. From Bimini to Eleuthera was another 160 miles.

Once I anchored off Eleuthera, I would be just one more American hanging out on his boat. A big speedboat was tempting from the standpoint of reducing travel time, but that would mean stopping for fuel *en route* and staying in a marina once I got to Eleuthera. Living on a go-fast boat for several days at anchor might get me noticed. It was a little unusual. Staying in a marina sacrificed my anonymity; I would be forced to deal with other people.

If I bought a beat-up sailboat, anyone who noticed me would write me off as just another boat bum. Boats like that were easy enough to come by; I could buy one for a few thousand dollars if I kept the length under 30 feet. The weather was settled this time of year, and I wasn't crossing an ocean. A nondescript boat that was moderately seaworthy would serve me well.

Buying from an individual seller and paying cash, I would leave no trace. Once I accomplished my mission, I could ditch the boat — even just abandon it — and be long gone before there were questions about transfer of title or registration with the authorities in Florida.

Finished with my second beer, I thought about Mary again. Too bad she wouldn't be working with me on this hit. It was the kind of thing she would enjoy. I thought again about sending her a message, but I vetoed the idea. When she was finished with whatever she was doing, she would let me know.

Powering on my laptop, I searched the online listings for sailboats in the Miami area for sale by owner. I was overwhelmed in a few minutes. There were plenty of choices, but having done this before, I could weed out most of them. I made a short list of three boats and jotted down the phone numbers and the details.

I glanced at the clock; it was too late to call. Setting the alarm for 7 o'clock, I went to bed, planning an early start in the morning.

9

THE FIRST BOAT I CALLED ABOUT WAS ON A TRAILER IN THE OWNER'S backyard. It was an old Morgan 30, a racer/cruiser from the early '70s. I knew the design; it was solid enough for my purposes, but it only took a few questions for me to cross it off my list. The boat spent the last three years out of the water. The owner swore it was seaworthy, but I knew what happened to boats that sat in some-body's backyard for three years. She might be a good deal for someone, but not for me. It would take at least a few days to get her ready for sea, even if she were perfect. At a minimum, I would have to get rid of all the insects and rodents, and the engine would need to be commissioned and serviced. I thanked the man for his time and hung up the phone.

The second one sounded promising. She was a 1972 Ericson 29. The owner said he bought her in rough shape 2 years earlier and sailed her most weekends. He was asking $6,500 — well within my price range. Money wasn't really an issue, but I wanted to keep it under $10,000 to avoid any banks having to report the transaction.

"What's rough shape mean to you?" I asked.

"Cosmetics," he said. "She's a solid little boat. The exterior's rough, and the interior... Do you know these boats?"

"Sort of," I said. "I've been aboard them over the years, but I've never owned one. What about the interior?"

"I bought her to race, figuring I would fix her up. My wife always wanted to try racing. She's hooked now, but she wants a newer boat. The cushions on this one are rotten, the veneer in the interior's all peeling, and some of the plywood in the furniture is delaminating from leaks over the years. But the old Ericsons were built like tanks. You could sail her anywhere, take off this afternoon, if you wanted to. Making her pretty is more effort than she's worth, at least to me."

"Where is she?" I asked.

"I keep her on a mooring off the Miami Yacht Club. You want to see her? I'm not working today, so I could meet you there if you're in the area."

"Yes," I said. "I'm about ten minutes from the Miami Yacht Club. You have a dinghy there?"

"Yep. Part of the package, if you want it. It's not much to look at, but it gets the job done. It'll take me about 20 minutes to get there."

"Good enough," I said. "Should I wait outside, or what?"

"Nah, go on inside. The club's not busy on a weekday morning. There's a squawk box at the gate. Tell 'em you're meeting Jack Schmidt and have a seat in the bar. Grab a cup of coffee, and I should be there before you finish."

Schmidt was right on time; he walked up and introduced himself. I left my sour coffee on the table and pulled out my wallet, heading to the bar. Schmidt waved off my effort to pay and called out, "Put it on my tab, Julie."

The girl nodded as we walked outside to the dinghy racks. Schmidt tugged an old Avon inflatable from the rack and let it flop on the ground. It looked like it was made from patches, but when he poked it, it was tight.

"Looks like crap, but it holds air," he said. "Drag it on down to the water; the kicker's in the shed. I'll go get it."

Once I got the dinghy to the water, I stopped and sat down on one of the tubes, taking off my shoes and socks. I tossed them in the dinghy as he approached carrying a beat-up old two-horse-power Yamaha.

He clamped the outboard on the transom and we pushed the dinghy out into the water. I stood holding the bow, the wavelets lapping against my lower shins. He fiddled with the outboard for a few seconds and gave the starter cord a pull. The engine sputtered to life on his first try.

Reading the surprise on my face, he grinned and yelled, "Cranks like that every time."

I nodded and pushed the dinghy out as I climbed in and sat on the opposite tube from him. He steered through the anchorage until we came to a battle-scarred, chalky-looking white fiberglass sailboat with faded, mismatched sail covers. I eyed what I could see of the waterline. The bottom paint looked fresh and free of growth, consistent with his weekend racing. The name on the transom was *Narnia*.

As Schmidt tied off the dinghy, I climbed aboard and took a turn around the deck, tugging on the stainless-steel standing rigging. She was all tuned up; everything felt good.

Schmidt unlocked the companionway and took out the drop boards. He sat on the cockpit coaming, watching me, a smile on his face.

When he saw me looking at the bare headstay, he said, "There was a junky roller furling headstay when I bought her. I trashed that and spent the money on three good headsails instead of replacing it. There's a 150, a 100, and a storm jib in bags in the forepeak. Never got around to rigging her for a spinnaker. The main is new — three reef points. Like I said, she's ready to go anywhere, as long as you aren't picky about her looks."

"How about the engine?" I asked. "An Atomic four?"

"No, the former owner put a little Yanmar diesel in. That's one reason I bought her. I never liked those old Atomic fours. Every one I ever messed with leaked gasoline. Dependable, but dangerous."

"Yeah," I said, climbing down the companionway.

"Look her over," he said. "I'll stay up here out of the way, but holler if you have a question."

"Thanks," I said, as I took in the area below deck.

His description was accurate; it was in rough shape, but clean. There were three sails in bags in the forepeak. I opened the bags and exposed enough of each to see that they were relatively new, in good condition. I went into the head and pumped the flush handle on the commode a few strokes, watching as the murky seawater from the anchorage rinsed the bowl.

"Holding tank?" I asked, raising my voice a little.

"Yeah, with a Y-valve. She's legal, but the tank's awful small. Same with the fresh water tank. There's only like 12 or 15 gallons of fresh water capacity."

"That's typical," I said, taking the battered plywood cover off the engine compartment. I studied the little diesel for a minute or two, looking for leaks. I didn't find any. Pulling out the dipstick, I found the oil level between the marks. I raised the dipstick to my nose and sniffed. Sweet; there was no diesel fuel in the crankcase.

"Fire her up, please," I said.

Schmidt reached for the instrument panel. "Here goes."

The little engine roared to life at his first touch of the key. I put the cover back on, but it was still noisy. I poked my head through the companionway and drew my hand across my throat.

When the engine went quiet, I asked, "Does the stove work?"

"Yeah, about as well as you can expect. It's alcohol, probably original."

"Ground tackle?" I asked.

Schmidt stood up and opened the cockpit locker, waving me up to look. "Twenty-five pound plow, 25 feet of chain, 200 feet of half-inch nylon three-strand," he said.

"I'll take her," I said. "Wire transfer to your bank okay? We can do it while you wait."

"You don't want a sea trial?"

I shook my head. "You have the paperwork?"

"In my car," Schmidt said. "The club manager's a notary."

"Okay. Let's go ashore and get this done," I said.

"All right."

A few minutes later, we sat in the club manager's office. Schmidt signed the back of the title and a blank bill of sale that the club manager tore from a pad, and the manager notarized both of his signatures.

"I didn't get your name, except for Finn," Schmidt said. "That first, or last?"

"Just leave it blank," I said. "It's going to be a gift for my nephew, but I don't know how my sister and her husband will want it registered. Insurance, you know?"

"Okay," Schmidt said. "You don't need to do a wire transfer; a personal check's okay."

"No problem," I said. "It's all set."

I took out my Phorcys phone and called a number from the directory. Phorcys handled their own wire transfers; I wasn't sure how it worked, but it did. When a woman answered with an extension number, I said, "Hi, it's Finn. That wire transfer we talked about earlier? It's for $6,500, to Jack Schmidt. He's here with me. I'll put him on and he can give you his account details."

I gave the phone to Schmidt, and he answered a few questions for her. After a minute, he looked surprised and glanced at me. "You want to talk to Finn?" he asked. After a couple of seconds, he turned to me. "She says we're done, unless you need something else."

I took the phone and thanked her, then disconnected the call.

"She said I should call my bank and verify that the money's there," Schmidt said.

I nodded. "I'll wait, just in case."

He took out his cellphone and placed the call. It took a minute for him to work through the menu to get a human on the other end. Once he explained what he needed, he waited a few seconds, grinned, and said, "No, that's all I need. Thanks."

"Man, that's slick," Schmidt said. "Congratulations on your new boat. You can leave it on the mooring for a while. I can call you when I get another boat. I have your number from when you called me this morning."

"Thanks, Jack. But I'll get her out of your way later today. Good luck finding your next boat. It's been a pleasure." I picked up the papers and stood.

"When you come back," the manager said, "just tell whoever answers the intercom at the gate that you're here for *Narnia*. I'll let the staff know. And if you have any trouble with the boat, I'll give you a hand with whatever you need." He handed me a business card.

"Good enough," I said. "Thanks, gentlemen."

I STOPPED at a grocery store and a marine supply store on my way back to the hotel. My trip to the Bahamas should be short; I kept the hotel room and my rental car, in case anybody was checking up on me. Besides, that saved me taking everything with me. If things went as I expected, I might lose the boat on my way back.

At the hotel, I lugged my purchases up to my room and packed everything into two new waterproof duffle bags — one for groceries and one for everything else. I would eat from cans for the next few days, unless I found a restaurant in the Bahamas.

Satisfied with my inventory, I hefted the bags, testing their weight. They were manageable. I slung the strap of one over my left shoulder and picked up the other one. I left my room and locked it, holding the key in my hand. When I set the bags in the trunk of the rental car, I unzipped one and put the room key in it.

Leaving the rental car in long-term parking at the Miami airport would provide more misdirection for anyone keeping tabs on me. On the way there, I stopped at a print-and-ship store in a strip shopping center. In my laptop, there were encrypted files to produce several useful forged documents. Today, I needed a U.S. Coast Guard Vessel Documentation Certificate for *Narnia* with an owner's name matching my current identity. I took the laptop inside and logged onto the store's Wi-Fi. Filling in the blanks on the form, I sent the output to a color laser printer.

I retrieved my form and paid the fee. *Narnia's* new document might not stand up to a forensic examination, but it was good enough to get me through customs in Bimini. I put the form with my other paperwork and stowed it with the laptop in one of my duffel bags.

Twenty minutes later, I pulled into the long-term parking lot at the airport; traffic was light in the middle of the day. I retrieved my two bags from the trunk and caught the shuttle bus to the main terminal. I walked through the departures area and caught the escalator down to baggage claim. Following the signs to ground transportation, I got in the taxi queue. The trip to the yacht club took about 15 minutes. I paid the driver and walked through the gate, following a member's car.

I was pleased that I didn't have to call for admittance; that was one less contact that could pin down my itinerary. There was no reason to think anyone was watching, but old habits die hard. Besides, in my line of work, you just never knew.

The tattered inflatable was tied to the club's dinghy dock where I asked Schmidt to leave it when we came ashore a couple of hours ago. I dropped my two duffle bags in the dinghy and fired up the outboard. When I got to *Narnia,* I tied the dinghy alongside and set the bags on the side deck.

I climbed aboard and took the bags below, stashing them in the forepeak. While I was there, I positioned the 150 percent jib under the forward hatch and went back on deck. Opening the hatch from above, I pulled the bagged sail through the opening of the hatch and set it on the foredeck.

It was time to bring the dinghy aboard. I freed the main halyard and hooked its snap shackle to my belt. Stepping over the side into the dinghy, I fastened the halyard's snap shackle to the D-ring on the dinghy's bow. I unclamped the outboard from the stern and set it on *Narnia's* side deck.

Climbing back aboard the big boat, I untied the dinghy's painter and used the halyard to hoist the dinghy aboard. I opened the air valves, and while the air hissed from the dinghy, I took the outboard back to its storage mount on the stern rail, clamping it in place. Returning to the dinghy, I rolled it up, forcing the last of the air from it. I bundled it up and lashed it to the cabin top in front of the mast.

Back in the cockpit, I opened the port locker and found the dipstick for *Narnia's* fuel tank. The dipstick was hanging next to a deck-plate key. Using the key, I unscrewed the deck-plate marked "Fuel" and checked the level. The 25-gallon tank was full. That would give me a range under power of close to 300 miles. With a decent sailing breeze, I wouldn't need more fuel for a round trip to Eleuthera. If I were forced to motor rather than sail, I could fill up at Chubb Cay, on the east side of the Bahama Bank.

I started the engine and let it idle while I uncovered the mainsail. Once I stowed the cover, I went up on the foredeck and hanked the jib onto the headstay, ready to hoist. I rigged the jib sheets and clipped the jib halyard to the head of the sail. Stepping back to the mast, I raised the mainsail, pausing for a moment to study it. Seeing that the reefing line was rigged through the first reef point, I nodded.

With a last look around to make sure I didn't forget anything, I went forward and dropped the mooring pennant. The light northwest wind blew *Narnia's* bow off to port as I scrambled back to the cockpit. At the helm, I shifted into forward gear and opened the throttle.

With the mainsheet running free, I let the mainsail flog while I threaded my way through the other moored boats. Once in the clear, I hauled in the sheet, feeling the boat heel as the mainsail began to draw. Motorsailing out of the anchorage, I rounded Watson Island and turned into the main ship channel, heading east. In a few minutes, I was in the ocean.

Bimini is a little over forty miles due east of Miami, but crossing the Gulf Stream at a 90-degree angle on a slow-moving sailboat makes it seem farther. As I left the coast of Florida behind, the wind shifted to a steady 12 knots from the west-south-west, an ideal breeze for my trip. *Narnia* rode the gentle swell at about 5 knots through the water. Looking at my handheld GPS showed that I was being set to the north at 3 to 4 knots by the Stream's current. Without steering to correct for that, I would miss Bimini by miles.

A little vector math told me I should correct my course by steering roughly to the southeast. This was no surprise; it's well known to sailors along Florida's east coast. My velocity made good to Bimini would be between three and four knots, assuming the wind held. It was late afternoon, now; I would be in Bimini early tomorrow morning.

Stopping to check in with Bahamian customs in Bimini meant I wouldn't make it to Eleuthera until sometime the day after tomorrow. By then my target, John Hawkins, would be settled in his compound. That should increase his vulnerability, so I wasn't too worried about the delay.

Once I left Bimini, I could lash the tiller and catnap until I was across the Bahama Bank. There was too much traffic in the Gulf Stream for me to risk napping this evening, but I would be well-rested by the time I got to Eleuthera. I should arrive in time to scope out his defenses in daylight. I would do my work the evening of my arrival and be underway for Miami by daylight the next morning.

10

MY STOP IN BIMINI TO CLEAR CUSTOMS WENT AS I EXPECTED IT would. An hour later, I was on my way across the Bahama Bank. It was early the next afternoon when I anchored between Porgy Point and Sandy Cay on the west side of Eleuthera. My trip from Bimini was an easy one, with a nice, steady breeze.

To my surprise, there were no other anchored boats within sight. Lady Luck was smiling on me. Most cruising boats anchored in Governor's Harbor or Rock Sound, both of which offered all-around protection from wind shifts.

My spot was about midway between the more popular anchorages, and it was exposed to the west. That was all right; the weather was settled, and there was a nice steady southeasterly wind. I didn't plan to be here for long.

I inflated the dinghy and launched it, tying it alongside while I retrieved the outboard from the stern rail. I put the outboard on the side deck and climbed down into the dinghy.

Once I clamped the outboard on the transom, I fired it up and went exploring. I poked along the shore until I found a sandy spot where I could beach the dinghy and secure it to a good-sized piece of driftwood.

Walking along the shore to the north, I came to a sandy road and followed it to the east. The island of Eleuthera was about a half-mile wide at this point. I walked across to the protected water of Savannah Sound. There's a settlement by that name, as well as the body of water. I crossed the main part of the island about a half-a-mile north of what passed for downtown Savannah Sound.

The Sound itself was a narrow body of shallow water, about two thousand yards wide. It was separated from the open ocean by a two-mile-long, narrow peninsula. The peninsula was less than 150 yards across for most of its length. The target's compound was on the north end of the peninsula; I could see it well enough from where I stood.

Access to the compound from land would involve a trek of roughly three miles from where I stood. The route would take me through the most populated parts of the area. My plan was to swim across the Sound; I could bypass the wall that separated the target's compound from its neighbors by doing that. Using a camera with a telephoto lens, I studied the compound. There was no sign of life, but I was looking at the back side of the villa. It faced the ocean on the other side of the peninsula.

Phorcys provided me with detailed aerial photographs of the north end of the peninsula, including the target's villa. What I could see matched what I expected. This was an isolated spot; Hawkins might not feel the need for sophisticated electronic security. From what I could tell, the gate in the wall was closed, secured with a chain. There was no guard there, but a man like Hawkins could have a few thugs with him for security. From my briefing, I knew to expect two or three armed men. Hawkins might have a woman with him, but I wouldn't know until I was inside his perimeter.

Not wanting to attract attention, I moved on, walking south along the waterfront of the Sound for a few hundred yards.

Before reaching the town, I turned west onto another sandy street. In less than a minute, I reached Queen's Highway, the main north-south road that followed the island's spine. I walked north along the highway until it intersected the road I took to reach the Sound when I first arrived. I followed it back to the west shore of the island and strolled along the water's edge until I reached my dinghy.

Back aboard *Narnia*, I rummaged in the cockpit locker until I found a small tarp I noticed when Jack Schmidt showed me the anchor before I bought the boat. I stretched the tarp over the boom, rigging it to shade the cockpit from the blistering sun. Retrieving a bottle of water from below, I settled in the cockpit to rest and wait for darkness to fall. I felt a little sleepy, so I set an alarm on my phone for midnight, just in case.

WHEN MY ALARM WENT OFF, it took me a moment to remember where I was. As consciousness returned, I sat up and looked around. There was enough moonlight to let me see that I was still alone in the anchorage. I went below and splashed water on my face as I collected my thoughts.

No people were out and about when I was ashore earlier, so I didn't expect to see anyone in the wee hours of the morning. Still, I took a lightweight, black neoprene wetsuit from my duffle bag and put it on. Aside from camouflage, it would provide protection from the sharp coral I would encounter on my swim across Savannah Sound.

I buckled a waterproof pouch around my waist and picked up my snorkel, mask, and flippers. The pouch held a razor-sharp folding combat knife, as well as a garrote fashioned from a stainless-steel-wire fishing leader. An inexpensive cellphone with a camera that didn't have an infrared filter was in there, as well.

Using the phone's camera, I could spot infrared beams that might trigger intrusion alarms at the target's villa.

Ready, I went up on deck and stepped down into the dinghy. After a moment's reflection, I opted to swim ashore instead. The distance was short, and the outboard was noisy enough that it might attract attention. Even though I didn't see any people earlier, there was no point in taking the risk of waking a light sleeper somewhere nearby. I was going to get wet anyway. I sat down in the dinghy and put on my snorkeling gear. Rolling over the side without making a big splash, I swam ashore. Taking off the snorkeling gear, I clipped it to a big carabiner on the belt that held my pouch.

I kept to the shadows along the side of the road as I crossed the island. Within ten minutes, I waded into the rougher water of Savannah Sound. The inlet from the open ocean was less than half a mile from where I stood. The ocean swell rolled in, piling up in the shallows. That was good. The sloppy waves would provide cover as I made my way across to Hawkins's compound.

This afternoon, I noticed from the wave pattern in the Sound that there was a reef stretching across the sound from shore to shore. With my dive booties to protect my feet, I could wade most of the way across. I left my mask and the heel straps of my flippers hooked to the carabiner and worked my way out onto the reef. The water wasn't as deep as I expected it would be, barely coming above my knees.

Wading while keeping a low profile was tough, given the wave action. After being knocked down a couple of times, I crept into the deeper water on the side of the reef away from the inlet. With the reef between me and the ocean, the sea state was a little smoother. I put the flippers on and swam along the back side of the reef. When I got to the opposite shore, I hooked the flippers back on my belt and waded along the shoreline in a crouch until I was past the wall that protected Hawkins's compound.

Taking my infrared detector/cellphone from the pouch, I made sure there were no IR beams that might trigger a perimeter alarm. There could be more sophisticated alarm systems, but it wasn't likely. Pressure sensors would be hard to install, given that the ground was mostly coral rock, and motion sensors would be prone to false alarms with all the windblown spray in the air. The villa was only a few feet above sea level, and the waves broke on the ocean beach just yards away.

I found a spot in the rocky area just inside the wall to stash my snorkeling gear, and then began to move toward the back side of the villa in a low crawl. The surface of the ground was peppered with razor sharp pieces of broken coral; I was glad for my wetsuit, booties, and diving gloves.

The surveillance photos Phorcys provided during my briefing showed that the living spaces of the villa all had floor-to-ceiling sliding glass doors opening onto a large patio that faced the beach. The back wall, the one facing me, had a few windows up high for light and ventilation. There were roll-down, steel hurricane shutters to protect the glass doors in the front wall. That also provided protection from unauthorized entry when the villa was unoccupied.

Once I was close to the back wall, I stood, stretching my cramped muscles for a moment. Taking the folding knife from my belt pouch, I crept along the back wall of the villa. At the northwest corner, I turned and followed the north wall. The master bedroom suite was at the northern end of the villa; as soon as I turned the next corner, I would be in plain sight from Hawkins's bed, based on the photo reconnaissance.

My last intelligence from Phorcys indicated that I could expect to find Hawkins alone with his mistress. There were servants, but they didn't live in. There might or might not be two bodyguards. If they were there, they stayed in a small room in the back part of the house, near the kitchen and storage areas. Access to their quarters would be through the living room, which was next door to Hawkins's bedroom.

I reached the front corner and leaned my head around, checking the patio. It was clear of people, and there were no lights showing from inside. Leaning farther around, I could see into the master bedroom suite. The glass doors were wide open. There was little furniture, aside from a king-size bed, low to the ground. A waist-high partition in the back corner of the room separated a bathroom area from the rest of the space, but there were no interior doors.

If there were security guards, and if something alerted them, they would have to enter through the glass doors. With luck, I could take out Hawkins without disturbing them. The woman sleeping next to Hawkins was a different problem. For her sake, I hoped she was a heavy sleeper.

Dropping to my hands and knees, I crawled around the corner and into the bedroom. Feeling my way, I found an empty liquor bottle on the floor. That was a positive sign. Maybe they were both smashed. As I moved into the room, the woman rolled onto her back and began to snore, the heavy, gurgling snore of a drunk.

Hawkins stirred. I froze, watching as he rolled onto his side, facing toward the woman. He reached for her, shoving her roughly. She lay like a rag doll as he turned her onto her side. She never woke up, but she did stop snoring.

Hawkins rolled onto his back and lay still. I watched, waiting to see if he dropped back off to sleep. After about a minute, he pivoted to a sitting position, putting his feet on the floor. He stood and shuffled into the bathroom area, where he began to relieve himself.

Gathering my feet under me, I moved toward him as fast and silently as I could. I wrapped my left arm around his neck from behind, driving my knife into his right kidney as he stiffened and started to struggle. Before he actually moved, he gasped and collapsed against me as my knife found its mark.

Bracing myself to take his weight, I held him erect, my left arm still locked around his throat. I waited a couple of minutes, frozen, counting off the seconds, until I was sure he was gone. Then I lowered him to the floor and left as quietly as I had come.

11

Leaving Eleuthera at 3 a.m., I made good time on my way back to Florida. Once I was on the Bahama Bank, I took advantage of the southeast wind to head for South Riding Rock. Leaving the shallows of the Bank and entering the Gulf Stream there gave me a much more favorable course to Miami than leaving from Bimini. Since no outbound customs clearance was required, I was able to just keep sailing.

My course to Miami from South Riding Rock was west-north-west, so the Gulf Stream gave me a boost instead of slowing me down. Forty hours after I left Eleuthera, I was about ten miles from the main ship channel into Miami. I held my course for Miami for another hour and then started my preparations to abandon ship.

Not wanting to deal with bringing *Narnia* back to the U.S., I planned to scuttle her about five miles offshore. The depth was close to 1,000 feet; she wouldn't pose any risk to other vessels. I would cover the last few miles in the dinghy and then puncture it and set it adrift.

I hove to and launched the inflatable. The seas were relatively calm, but it was still a challenge to get the outboard clamped on the dinghy's stern. Once I had the dinghy ready, I went below and got the waterproof duffle bag I planned to take with me. The other bag had a few groceries left in it; it would go down with the ship. I took the duffle bag up on deck and dropped it into the dinghy.

Opening the cockpit locker, I crawled down into the space below the cockpit and closed the seacocks for the engine seawater intake and the cockpit drains. Using the serrated back edge of my combat knife, I sawed through the hoses that were connected to the seacocks.

I climbed back up on deck and went forward. I cut the lashing that held the anchor in place on the bow roller. Folding the knife, I put it in my pocket, retrieving my multi-tool. Using the pliers from the multi-tool, I unscrewed the pin from the shackle that held the anchor to its 30 feet of chain.

I pulled the rest of the chain out of the hawse pipe, piling it on deck. Swapping the multi-tool for my knife, I cut the rope anchor rode free from the chain. I dragged the chain back to the side deck and fed it over the toe rail into the dinghy. Its weight would help sink the dinghy when the time came.

Taking the anchor with me, I went below deck and slashed the drain hoses under the head sink. Seawater gushed in through the two open seacocks. Going aft to the galley, I opened the cabinet under the sink and cut the big hose leading from the sink drain to another seacock. More seawater poured in. I heard the automatic bilge pump start running as the seawater flooded the bilge sump.

In the main cabin, I opened the storage bins under the settees, exposing the inner surface of the fiberglass hull. Swinging the twenty-five pound anchor like a sledgehammer, I smashed several fist-sized holes in the hull on each side. The seawater rushed in, flooding the storage compartments.

I scurried back up on deck and dropped the anchor into the inflatable dinghy — more ballast to make sure that it would sink

when I wanted it to. Ducking into the still-open cockpit locker, I
opened the three seacocks I closed a few minutes earlier. I was
soaked by the rush of water before I could climb out.

Back in the cockpit, I leaned down to the instrument panel
and switched off the bilge pump. Satisfied that *Narnia* would soon
be gone, I climbed down into the dinghy and cast off, starting the
outboard and heading for the lighted entrance to the ship
channel.

I glanced over my shoulder periodically, checking on *Narnia*.
She was settling quickly; she would be gone before I got ashore.

An hour later, I maneuvered the dinghy into the corner
between the riprap on the north side of Government Cut and the
southernmost part of Miami Beach. When I was as close to the
beach as I dared go with the outboard still running, I put the nose
of the dinghy up against the rip-rap. The thrust of the engine
would hold the dinghy there for a moment.

I set my duffle bag on the broken rock of the riprap and took
out my trusty knife. I punctured both air chambers of the dinghy
and scrambled up onto the rocks, the dinghy's painter in my
hand.

Grabbing the bow of the dinghy, I pushed and shoved until I
turned it around. Then I tossed the painter into it. I watched for a
few seconds as it motored out to sea at about a 45-degree angle to
the beach. With any luck, it would make it into deeper water
before it lost its buoyancy and sank.

Slinging the duffle bag's strap over my shoulder, I climbed
over the rocks and made my way into South Pointe Park. It was
almost midnight, but I soon found an idle taxi to take me to the
airport where I left my rental car.

I considered checking in with Phorcys to report that my
mission was a success, but decided that could wait until I had a
good night's sleep. Besides, they probably already knew; Hawkins
would have been found two days ago. Sailing played tricks on my
sense of time.

BY THE TIME I retrieved my rental car from the airport parking lot and got back to my hotel room, it was almost one o'clock. A quick look around satisfied me that the room wasn't disturbed while I was in the Bahamas, except for maid service. The bed was made the morning after I left, and there were fresh towels in the bathroom. My soft-sided suitcase was as I left it, not that there was anything of value in it.

Dropping my duffle bag, I went in the bathroom and turned on the shower to let the water get hot. I stripped off my salt-crusted clothes and tossed them in the tub so they would get rinsed while I cleaned myself up.

I stepped into the shower, enjoying the cascades of hot, fresh water. Once my hair and skin no longer felt salty, I lathered my face and shaved while letting the water hammer my shoulders and neck. Clean at last, I shut off the water and grabbed a towel. Living on a small sailboat, I was used to being salty most of the time. Being used to it doesn't mean I like it; it just heightens my appreciation for a hot, freshwater shower.

Dry and clean for the first time in days, I slipped between the crisp, fresh sheets and closed my eyes. I don't know how long I slept before I found myself awake and alert. I lay still, keeping my eyes closed and my breathing even while I assessed my surroundings.

The room was still dark, and the air conditioner's fan was blowing steadily, masking the occasional sound of passing cars outside. The refrigerator in the minibar was humming, then it stopped. Nothing seemed amiss. I opened my eyes to slits, looking around the darkened room as best I could without moving my head. There was a pool of deeper shadows in the corner between the entry door and the door to the connecting room. That dark area was new; it wasn't there when I fell asleep.

I sensed movement in that corner. Tensing my muscles

without moving more than necessary, I made sure my limbs were ready for use. In one violent movement, I lurched from the bed. I swept my folding combat knife from the nightstand and popped the blade open with my thumb as I rushed the shape in the corner.

My right leg gave way as I put my weight on it. I felt a bare foot hook the back of my calf as my leg folded at the knee, and I crashed to the floor. I twisted as I fell, swinging the knife in a wide arc without making contact. As I recoiled and gathered myself for another lunge, the intruder spoke.

"Take it easy, sailor. It's just me."

"Mary?" I asked, as she flipped the light switch by the entry door.

"I've missed you," she said. "Sorry I woke you; I was planning a different kind of arousal."

My eyes adjusting to the light, I saw that she was as naked as I was. "I see," I said.

I unlocked the blade and folded the knife, putting it on the nightstand behind me as she put her arms around my neck. I reached around her and turned the light off.

LATER, as we lay side by side catching our breath, I asked, "How did you get in here? The chain's on the door."

"I booked the adjoining room. I came through the connecting door."

"Oh," I said, thinking. "But it's locked from this side."

She giggled. "Normally, yes. But you left a key to this room at the desk for me, remember?"

"So you got the key and opened the connecting door."

"Yes."

"Why did you do that? You could have just waited in here for me. Why did you book the adjoining room?"

"I wanted to be sure it was you. Somebody could have taken the key away from you and come to search the room."

I nodded. "Okay. You're a little late for our rendezvous."

"You weren't sitting here waiting for me, Finn. I've been here for two days."

"I was expecting you over a week ago. There were jobs to do; I couldn't put things on hold indefinitely."

"Sorry," she said. "My personal business took a little longer than I expected. I left you a message in the email drop."

"I know. I got it. The voice mail, too."

"You didn't answer the email; that worried me."

"I didn't know what to tell you, especially after that voice mail. Besides, you were busy with your friend Louie and his pals."

"That wasn't what it looked like, Finn."

"No?"

"No. I was setting something up."

"That *is* what it looked like, Mary. Like you were setting something up with Kyle Brandon, from what I heard."

"How did you... You didn't follow us into the Pink Parrot. I was watching for that."

"I didn't need to. That place is well-known for shady business. It wasn't hard to find out who your pimp friend hooked you up with."

"Finn?"

"Yes?"

"What do you think you know about what I was doing?"

I shook my head. "I don't want to play that game with you again. I thought we were past that, after all the lies you told me to begin with. I'm not going back there."

"You're angry," she said.

"I could get there, for sure. But I'm not angry yet. Let's just say I'm cautious about trusting you, again."

She nodded her head. "Not without reason. I wish I could start over with you, knowing what I know now."

"Yeah, well, that's not the way life works. If you want to start over, you have to start from where we are now."

"I'll try, Finn. Where should I start? From when you saw me with Louie Rayburn?"

"How about from when you got off the plane here a couple of weeks ago and missed your check in with Phorcys?"

"Okay. I can do that. Before I do, though, I want you to know that I didn't just blow off Phorcys. I squared this with them."

"Isn't that part of what you need to tell me about your activities since you stepped off the plane?"

"Yes, I suppose it is. This will be embarrassing for me, Finn, what I have to tell you. I've never told anybody most of what I'm going to tell you. I don't even admit a lot of it to myself. You understand?"

"I think so. You don't have to tell me, if it's too painful."

"Where would that leave us? You and me, I mean?"

"Where we are, I guess."

"I don't like where we are," Mary said.

"No. I don't either."

"Then I guess I have to tell you everything. I feel like I'm taking a huge risk, doing that."

"I don't understand."

"You'll hear some ugly stuff about me. What if you're so repulsed that you want nothing further to do with me, Finn? Then what? I don't..."

"Mary, I can't give you an honest answer to that without knowing what you're going to tell me. I understand the risk you'd be taking. I can't give you the reassurance you're looking for. You must see that. You've got a pretty good handle on me and how I look at things. Make a judgment about how I'll react and take your chances. Or don't. That's your choice. If I told you anything else, it wouldn't be fair to either of us."

"Okay. Thanks for being straight with me. You're the best

thing that's ever happened to me, Finn. I love you. However this comes out, that won't change."

"I love you too, Mary. That's the best I can do, right now. I hope it's enough to get us through this; I sure as hell want it to be."

"There's one other thing, Finn. Before I start, can we get dressed? I know it sounds stupid, but..."

"I don't think it's stupid at all. There's naked, and then there's *naked*. I get that."

12

By the time we were both dressed, it was getting light outside. The gray light was leaking around the edges of the drapes when Mary asked, "Should I make a pot of coffee?"

"Sure," I said, "unless you want to go get breakfast."

A sad smile on her face, she said, "No, thanks. Later, maybe, but I need to get this over with."

She flipped the switch on the coffeemaker at the minibar and sat down in a chair at the small, round table. I took the other chair and caught Mary's eye. She held my gaze for a couple of beats and pulled her lips into a grimace. Then she spoke.

"This has to begin a little earlier than my arrival in Miami, if you want the full picture."

I nodded. "It's your story. Start wherever you want."

"I told you my mother was a single mom, and a drug addict, but I didn't tell you she was a prostitute."

"Those things sometimes go together."

"Yeah. Well, we lived in this slummy trailer park, the kind where nobody owns their own trailer. It was in a rough section on the outskirts of Miami. The whole area was overrun by gangs and ne'er-do-wells. I don't know who my father was. My mother probably didn't, either. A lot of my early childhood is lost to me. I just plain can't remember it.

"There were men coming and going at all hours of the night and day. Sometimes, they would wait their turn in the little den in the trailer. I guess it was meant to be a living room, but... That was my room, where I played and slept, so I was there while they waited. There were just the two rooms, and a bathroom. Plus a little galley-like kitchen. Most of the men ignored me. Some of them were nice to me. A few of them made me...do things. My mom knew about that; she knew which ones abused me. She made them pay extra."

Mary took a deep breath and let it out in a long sigh, shifting her gaze to the table top. The coffee was ready. She got up and poured a cup for each of us, bringing the cups back to the table. She sat down and took a sip of coffee. Glancing up at me for a moment, she dropped her eyes and spoke.

"Louie Rayburn was her pimp, but more than that. He owned the trailer. Several others in that trailer park, too. He would come around early in the morning, every morning, to collect whatever money she made. I don't know if she got to keep a little, like whatever she got for selling me, maybe. Or maybe it all went to Louie for drugs and rent and groceries. He would take her and a few other women away in his car every so often, and she would come back with bags from the grocery store. Louie brought her drugs each morning when he came to collect from her.

"As I got older, more of the men were interested in me. Some of them would come just to..." Mary shook her head and wiped at the tears running down her cheeks.

"She would get angry with me about that, call me a shameless little slut sometimes, like she was jealous. Other times, she beat me if I didn't come on to them and let them... Well, you get the picture. There was this one guy, a friend of Louie's. Anyhow, he had a special thing for me, and he liked...uh... He did things that hurt me. He was a sick bastard. Even as a kid I knew that.

"As I got older, I figured out I was better off staying the hell away from the trailer and taking my chances on the streets. I spent as little time as possible at my mother's, but I had nowhere else to go, really. I was maybe 12 years old when I came back and found her dead. I didn't know what to do. I called the cops. And I've told you about most of what happened after that."

She went into the bathroom and I heard her blowing her nose, and splashing water in the sink. On her way back to the chair, she picked up the coffee pot and refilled our cups. She sat down and took a sip of coffee.

Locking eyes with me, she said, "Okay, you've got the background. Fast forward to my arrival in Miami two weeks ago. I spotted Louie in the arrivals area, hustling this lost-looking young girl. She was dressed neatly, but a little ragged-looking, with an oversized backpack. I got close enough to listen to his spiel. She was broke and looking for help. You can guess what he was doing. In the end, it turned out she was too smart for him. That one got away, but I kept an eye on Louie. He was meeting flights that came from the places that college kids go when they're bumming around on their gap years, or whatever.

"It pissed me off that he was doing that. I've wanted to repay him for my lost childhood for a long time. So I changed clothes in a ladies' room, dressed myself to look like a college girl bumming around, and dropped the duffle bag at a baggage-hold booth. I took my backpack and went hunting. I figured that after 12 years, he wouldn't recognize me, and I was right."

Taking another sip of coffee, she continued her story. "I let him pick me up — gave him the same kind of sob story the other girl did. He bought it. Took me back to his place and fed me, let me get some rest. After a couple of days, he told me it was time for me to repay the favors. He wanted me to meet this 'friend' of his. He gave me hooker clothes to wear, in case I was too slow to figure out what he was planning. We got in this stretch Hummer with three of his goons and swung by an apartment in South

Beach. One of the goons went inside and came back with two other girls. The Hummer dropped us off at the Pink Parrot. That's when I spotted you watching the place. What were you doing there?"

"Staking it out. I was working a target for Phorcys. We knew the guy hung out there."

"Who?"

"I'll tell you about my adventures later. Finish your story."

She grimaced and nodded. "Okay. We went inside, and Louie's friend was at a table with two young guys. The friend was an up-and-coming politician. Louie told me if I hooked up with him, it could set me up for the long haul. I figured that was bullshit, but I played along, because I recognized the guy. He was the jerk who liked to sodomize me when I was a kid." She paused and looked up at me.

"But he didn't recognize you?"

"No. My appearance changed when I went through puberty, Finn. I was a skinny little waif back then. For all I knew, this perverted piece of shit wouldn't even go for an adult female. But I did have the advantage of knowing what his kinks were, so I could play him all right. He made a date with me for the next night at his office. By then, the other two girls were hooked up with the two young guys, so we left them there.

"Louie and his three trained gorillas took me back to his place. On the way, they told me all about how they would make sure I was properly 'broken in' for my big date the next evening. Gave me a lot of graphic detail about what it would take to please the guy, and how they would make sure I was all 'loosened up' for him. Jerks."

"So you went back to Louie's place. Then what?"

"I let them push me around until we were inside. While the four of them were shoving me back and forth and groping me, I got a gun away from one of them and kneecapped Louie. Then I killed the others and tied Louie to a chair. I worked on him for a little while; I wanted more information about my date for the next night."

She stopped and looked me in the eye for a few seconds. "You must have picked that up from the news; it was all they talked about that morning."

I nodded. "Yes, sure. What did you learn from Louie about the other guy?"

"He was Louie's supplier from way back. Connected to a Colombian cartel forever and paying off all kinds of people. I wouldn't be surprised if he was on O'Hanlon's list; he was the kind of person Phorcys would have tagged for us. Kyle Brandon was his name. His death made the news, too. Did you see any of that?"

"I've been out of the country for a few days," I said. "I didn't get much local news from the States. What happened?"

"He gave me his card at the Pink Parrot and told me to call him at around 5:30 to make sure he was alone in his office. I did, and when I got there, he let me in. I put the moves on him big time, convinced him to let me tie him up in his big leather swivel chair. Then I fixed him up with a Colombian necktie. While he was dying, I told him who I was. But I don't think the son of a bitch even remembered the little girl in the trailer."

"Anything else you need to tell me?"

"What more could I tell you?"

"I don't know; it's your story. Whatever you think I should know, I guess."

"There's not really any more, Finn. Unless you want the gory details of what my mother's johns did to me."

"I don't need that. But I'll listen, if you need to tell me."

She looked at me for a moment, collecting her thoughts. "No, I don't need to. I have to live with all the sick stuff I did, but you don't."

She put her face in her hands and sobbed. I got up and moved closer, dropping to my knees next to her chair. I put my arms around her and gave her a squeeze. She leaned against me, still crying. I patted her back and stroked her shoulder.

"Mary?" I asked, when she calmed a bit.

"It's okay, Finn. I know it's disgusting. I don't blame you."

"Don't blame me for what?"

"For wanting to ditch me."

"I don't want to ditch you. Don't do that to yourself."

"But I'm... I let them..."

"You were a child, Mary. Don't blame yourself for things you couldn't control."

"But maybe if I had — "

I gave her a gentle shake. "Stop it, now. Put it behind you. It's all in the past. We can't change the past, and you mustn't let it ruin our future."

"Our future?" she asked. "After all that, we have a future?"

"I sure hope so. If not, you'll break an old man's heart."

"You're not so old, Finn. You sure about this?"

"Yep. Never been more sure of anything in my life."

Mary wept freely and collapsed against my chest. I let her cry herself out. When she calmed down, I said, "There is one thing that worries me, though."

She pulled away, sitting up straight, frowning at me. "What?"

"Where do you stand with Phorcys?"

"I told you I squared this with them. Why do you ask? Have they..."

"I haven't talked to anybody there in a few days, but before I left on my last mission, Aaron said you still hadn't checked in; he kept asking me if you had been in touch with me since you got to Miami."

"Oh. He may know by now. Maybe not the details, but he'll know I'm still part of the team."

"Who did you talk with? Mike?"

She shook her head. "No. My uncle. I figured if anybody would understand, he would."

I forgot about that. Mary's uncle, Bob Lawson, her mother's older brother, was one of the founders of Phorcys, along with Mike Killington. Lawson was also the man who recruited me to work as part of his special projects team within the Department of Defense over 20 years ago. He tried to help Mary's mother get free of her demons, although she shut him out for whatever reason. Mary and I suspected that Lawson was behind hiring her to work for Phorcys, after she established herself as a freelance assassin.

"I'm not sure what he's told Aaron and Mike," Mary said. "By now, though, I'm sure he's let them know I'm still in the fold. I last talked with him the morning after I killed Brandon."

"What did you tell him about Rayburn and Brandon?"

"Just that I ran across two of the men who ruined my mother's life — and mine. I told him I needed to take the time to sort them out before I lost track of them."

"You didn't tell him who they were?"

"No. He didn't ask. Why?"

"When I saw you at the Pink Parrot, I was there on a stakeout, looking for my next assigned target."

"You said that. So?"

"So, my target was Kyle Brandon," I said. "You were right about him being on O'Hanlon's list."

"Then I saved you some work. Did you take credit for the hit?"

I chuckled. "No, Mary. I didn't. It doesn't pay to lie to people like Mike Killington and Bob Lawson."

"No, I agree. Now it's your turn to tell your story, though. What have you been up to while we were apart?"

"Well, I've been busy, but first, I want to compliment you on the Rayburn hit."

"What do you mean?"

"Well, I got Aaron to run the plates on the Hummer when I saw you get out of it. It was registered to Rayburn. Then I saw the news the next morning. It didn't take much thought to put the pieces together, especially when I heard about the hooker with the slit skirt on the news."

"You didn't tell him, did you? About me, I mean."

"No. Just about a guy who looked like a pimp taking three hookers into the club. I had a hunch that Brandon was already in there — don't know why I thought that. Rayburn made a big splash, so I wanted to know who he was. Besides, you were hanging out with him."

"Yeah, but now you know why."

"Yes, and you should know you did a first-rate job on Rayburn and his friends."

"Thanks, but I didn't get away as clean as I wanted to. You saw the news. That old bat who kept ranting about the slit in my skirt worried me. I don't know how she saw all of that. Maybe a security camera on the door of her unit. I was wearing a wig, but still..."

"Don't worry. You covered your tracks well. The cops put together a murder/suicide story based on the forensics. They figured the woman was full of shit, maybe making stuff up based on other times she saw Louie taking girls to his place. She was a chronic complainer, according to them. "

"I never got that from the news. What are you basing that on?"

"When Aaron told me who owned the Hummer, he mentioned that Rayburn was a political consultant. Since I was after Brandon and he was a politician, Aaron did more checking. He has a source inside the Pink Parrot. He got a rundown on the meeting between Rayburn and Brandon and the three hookers, including Brandon slipping you a note."

"You said you didn't tell Aaron I was involved."

"I didn't. You were described as the girl with the auburn hair. But I saw you get out of the Hummer, remember?"

"Right. Okay. Then what?"

"Then Aaron wanted to know more about the Rayburn hit. He got hold of the cops' murder book. You didn't leave any trace evidence, and they bought your setup. The only loose end was that they couldn't figure out why the one bodyguard who killed everybody tortured Rayburn. It didn't make sense, unless it was for revenge. He didn't do it for information, obviously, since he blew his own brains out right after he killed Rayburn."

Mary smiled. "Yeah, I worried about that. I wanted to pick Louie's brain about what to expect with Brandon. And just between you and me, maybe I enjoyed hearing the little shit screaming into the pillow while I crushed his fingers. I know that's not professional, but it was satisfying all the same. So the cops were right, in a way. Revenge *was* one motive for the torture."

"Fair enough," I said. "While we're still talking about you and Rayburn and Brandon, I was watching Brandon's campaign headquarters that night."

I told Mary about watching him close up shop and take a phone call before she showed up.

"That would have been my call," she said.

"I guessed that. Great disguise, by the way. I didn't know you were so good at that."

"Thanks. I minored in theater while I was getting my accounting degree. It comes in handy."

"Yeah, I can see that. I wouldn't have recognized you, except I suspected it might be you. The coincidence was too strong to overlook."

"What did you do, after he closed the blinds?"

"I waited. At that point, I didn't know for sure it was you. That was before I got the details on the Rayburn hit from Aaron, and from a distance, I didn't recognize you."

"But what about the coincidence?"

"I only discovered the coincidence later. I saw you take a négligée out of your briefcase, but I figured you and Brandon were just messing around on the side, or something."

"So you waited. How long?"

"Well, I was planning to kill him in his office, if I could get him alone there. I didn't see you come out, though. I waited maybe 10 minutes, I guess."

"And then what?" she asked.

"I caught a glimpse of you as you drove past me; I was in a car parked across the street from his office. I figured you must have left by a back door, so I went looking in the alley. I still didn't know it was you, though. When I found the door unlocked and got inside, I found him in his office. That's when everything fell into place for me."

"Shit," Mary said.

"What's wrong?"

"I didn't pick up on the surveillance. Good thing it was you and not a cop."

"Yeah, I guess. But a cop wouldn't have made the connections I did — wouldn't have had enough background."

"Maybe. I'm still disappointed in myself."

"It was a good, clean hit, Mary. Lighten up. And you know what's ironic?"

She shook her head. "What?"

"The Colombian necktie."

"Why is that ironic?"

"Because that was one option I considered for him, to make it look drug-related. But then I decided to make it look like a bungled burglary. I figured that would raise fewer questions."

That brought a smile to her face. "Great minds, and all that," she said. "Now, what have you done since you got to Miami besides spy on me? You said you were out of the country for a few days."

"Yes. I'll tell you all about it, but can we go get breakfast first? I missed dinner last night."

GIVEN that Mary and I needed a place where we could talk, we drove to South Beach and parked near Lincoln Road Mall. We strolled along until we spotted an upscale restaurant that wasn't crowded, and asked for a secluded table. The waiter brought us a pot of coffee and took our orders.

"Have you kept up with the national news?" I asked, as Mary stirred her coffee.

"More or less. Why?"

"Did you hear about the Secretary of Defense?"

"His heart attack?" she asked.

"That's the official word," I said.

"Was it something else?"

"You have to wonder. I mean, the news didn't mention it, but my whole chain of command got wiped out, starting with Nora. Or Phyllis — whatever her real name was."

Nora was my boss before Mary and I killed her. We were plotting to kill Nora's boss, a Deputy Secretary of Defense, when somebody beat us to him.

"There's not much of a pattern, Finn. Nora disappeared. Looks like the Russian Mafia got her boss. What I saw in the news was that the Secretary of Defense died in his sleep at his place near here. A woman on his staff showed up the next morning with some documents for him, and his Secret Service detail went to his bedroom to check on him. They thought he was sleeping in."

"Yeah, that was the story they fed the press, I guess. That's mostly right. Rumor has it that the woman who found him left him in bed asleep while she went to the bathroom. When she came back he was dead — cardiac arrest."

"Rumor, huh? Any reason to put your faith in that?" She smiled.

"It fits the facts as I know them."

"Okay. I wondered about that when I heard it. Potassium chloride?"

"Fits the facts," I said.

"And then you were watching the Pink Parrot for Brandon when you saw me. Was Rayburn somebody you were expecting?"

"Nope. Just Brandon. But I did ask Aaron to do a full workup on Rayburn. The last time I talked to him, he just had some basic info on him."

"You said you were out of the country for the last few days. Where?"

"The Bahamas," I said, pausing to let the waiter serve our breakfasts.

Once he refilled our coffee cups and left us alone, I resumed.

"I bought a little boat and took a sail. Round trip to Eleuthera."

"What took you there?"

"I wanted to meet a guy named John Hawkins. But he died about the time I got there, so I anchored for a few hours and came back."

"Still have the boat?"

"It sank in the Gulf Stream not far off Miami. I made it ashore in the dinghy."

"You've been busy. Did you miss me?"

"You know I did. I was worried about you."

"I'm sorry, Finn. Forgive me?"

"Of course. I understand how things like that go. I'm glad you're back with me."

"Me, too. What's next?"

"I need to check in with Aaron and let him know about Hawkins."

"You don't think he's heard? Wouldn't the news have picked that up?"

"Maybe not," I said. "It's been a couple of days, now. I'm sure the U.S. media will pick it up one of these days, but he was stabbed when he surprised an intruder in the middle of the night. The local police will try to keep it quiet. That kind of thing's not good for their tourist business."

Mary chuckled. "Was he alone?"

"Not exactly. There was a woman in the bed with him, but she was in a drunken stupor. Her snoring woke him up, and he went to the bathroom. That's where he got stabbed."

She laughed at that, a real laugh.

"What's so funny?"

"The symmetry. Sanders had a heart attack while his lady friend was in the bathroom. I never thought of going to the bathroom in the middle of the night as being dangerous, but I guess it is — to yourself and to your close friends."

I shook my head. "Let's finish breakfast. I want to talk with Aaron and see what's up next, since you're back in the game."

"What are you going to tell him about me?"

"I'll see if he mentions you, first. If he does, I'll be guided by what he says. If not, I'm not sure I should bring it up. You said your Uncle Bob was going to handle it, right?"

"Yes. Maybe I should give him a quick call when we get back to the room and see where he stands with it. Then you'll know what to expect."

"Good," I said. "You ready?"

"I am," Mary said. "Let's go."

I signaled our waiter for the check. When he brought it, I paid him in cash, with a generous tip.

13

BACK IN MY ROOM, MARY MADE HER CALL TO BOB LAWSON WHILE I took a quick shower. Their conversation was brief. She told me about it when I was dry and dressed.

"Uncle Bob's fixed it with Aaron. He told Aaron that I needed the time to handle some family matters. He asked Aaron to respect my privacy and told him that I would be in touch as soon as you and I reconnected. Bob thought it would be fine for both of us to call Aaron, and he knows I'm going to share this with you before we call."

"Good enough," I said. "Does he know about Rayburn and Brandon?"

"Bob?" she asked.

I nodded.

"No. Not from me, anyway. He didn't ask, and I didn't volunteer any names. Are you going to tell Aaron?"

"I don't see the point. Do you?"

"Not really, unless something else comes up. But I know you and Aaron are tight. If you think he needs to know, it's okay with me."

I shook my head. "I'm with Bob. We should respect your privacy. If something else comes up, you make the call."

"Thanks, Finn. For everything."

"Forget it. I'm just glad you're back. Let's make that call."

I turned the air conditioner's fan to the highest setting to provide some white noise. There was no reason to think anybody was eavesdropping on us, but you never knew. Using the encrypted iPhone provided by Phorcys, I called Aaron.

"Finn?" he answered.

"Yeah. I had a worthwhile trip to Eleuthera."

"Good. I gathered as much. We picked up on a robbery/murder report through a source in Nassau. They're keeping it extra quiet — bad for business. Where are you now?"

"I'm back at the hotel, with Mary."

"Put her on, then."

"Just a second." I switched the phone to speaker mode and set it on the table between us. I nodded at her. "Keep your voices down, both of you," I cautioned. "We're on the speaker."

"Hi, Aaron."

"Welcome back, Mary. We were worried about you, but Bob explained. Everything okay with you now?"

"Yes, thanks. It's good to be back."

"Good. Hey, Finn?"

"Yes?"

"Remember when you were wondering if Rayburn might be connected to more of O'Hanlon's organization? But maybe at a level below the one that was in O'Hanlon's records?"

"Yes. Why?"

"Have you shared that with Mary?"

"No. We haven't gotten a chance to get into that kind of detail. Why do you ask?"

"Never mind. You can fill her in later, but I swear, man, you're psychic. There's a whole 'nother layer; it's like peeling a damn onion. And remember our conversations about the 'mystery man?' The Russian who was trying to pick up the pieces of O'Hanlon's empire?"

"Yes. What's that got to do with Rayburn?"

"I'll get there. You got time? Or should we do this later?"

"We're not going anywhere. Now's good."

"Okay. Those three bodyguards of Rayburn's — I told you they were retired U.S. Marshals, right?"

"Yes."

I watched Mary's eyebrows rise when she heard that.

"Well," Aaron said, "it turns out that wasn't quite accurate. They were still active; working witness protection. The retired thing was part of the whole Rayburn cover story."

"Rayburn was in witness protection?" I asked.

"No. He was a confidential informant in that super-secret Department of Justice investigation I told you about."

"You told me about two super-secret DoJ investigations, Aaron. One into Senator Lee, and the other into the Russian mystery man. You weren't sure the two were related."

Early in my relationship with Mary, Senator Jefferson Davis Lee was involved in kidnapping my daughter. He was part of the O'Hanlon crime empire, and they were trying to force me to give up Mary and the incriminating records that she had stolen from O'Hanlon's bagman, but that's an old story. After O'Hanlon's demise, there were rumors that a mysterious Russian was trying to take over O'Hanlon's racket. There were indications that the Russian may have been working with O'Hanlon all along, too.

"Yeah," Aaron said. "Well, it's looking like those were two branches of the same investigation."

"I'm surprised somebody didn't shut down the DoJ, Aaron. I would have thought the fix was in. We know the Secretary of Defense was on the take. Why not the Attorney General? Or the — "

"Don't even think it, Finn. Let alone say it."

"I thought you said these funky phones you gave us were encrypted."

"Yeah. I'm not worried about the phone. It's just not good to think thoughts like that out loud. It scares me, that's all."

"You're right. Sorry."

"No sweat. Back to your question, we're still working on this. One school of thought is that the whole investigation is a coverup. They could have been using Rayburn as a conduit between the Russian and crooks in the government."

"That's an interesting thought. What other ideas are you working?"

"It's possible that the investigation itself is legit, but the fix is in elsewhere."

"How would that work?" I asked.

"Nobody's sure of anything, at this point. We need to keep all the options open, keep an open mind. We don't want to narrow our focus and miss something. I'll keep you posted on that."

"Any idea who put out the hit on Rayburn?" I figured a little misdirection wouldn't hurt anything.

"No, not yet. The cops still think it was murder/suicide, but our sources say the DoJ doesn't buy that. They're letting the cops' story stand in the interest of keeping things quiet, but we hear they're digging into the background of the one marshal who shot himself. Not sure what they're thinking there. Maybe that he wiped everybody else out and then somebody nailed him. But they can't make sense of who or how. The bad guys are convinced it was a hit too, but everybody's got a different idea of who to blame."

"And what about Brandon?"

"The cops are all over that one, but they don't have any ideas. Obviously, Brandon didn't cut his throat and pull his own tongue out through the slit. They've run through all his staffers. Most of them left the office together and went out for drinks that night, so they can alibi one another. The others all have good alibis, too.

They've canvassed the neighborhood, but that didn't go anywhere. You've seen that place. Not much going on there after 5 o'clock."

"No, it was pretty quiet. So they're stumped, huh?"

"Well, they found out Brandon and Rayburn met at the Pink Parrot the night before, like I told you. Those two new hires that Rayburn fixed up with the girls probably told the cops about the meeting. The cops talked to the two girls, but you can guess how that's going. The new hires and the waitress that was taking care of their table both mentioned a third girl. Interesting thing — her description matched the Wells woman's description of the hooker in the slit skirt. She left the Pink Parrot with Rayburn and his three bodyguards. Disappeared into thin air, unless you believe Mrs. Wells."

"It seems unlikely that Mrs. Wells would have made up a description that was such a good match for the girl Rayburn took to the Pink Parrot. Where are the cops going with that?" I asked, admiring Mary's poker face.

"Dead end, so far. Nobody noticed anything about her except the auburn hair and the skirt. They tracked down the other two hookers, but they swore they never saw her before that night. Said she was in the Hummer already when Rayburn and his goons picked them up. Ditto for the staff at the Pink Parrot. She wasn't one of their regular working girls."

"Are the cops still looking for her?" I asked.

"Theoretically, yeah. But not very hard. I mean, they've got a good story for Rayburn and his pals. They don't want to reopen the case. Could be Wells saw them drag the girl in on a different night, according to the cops. Could be it was the same night, and the girl left without Mrs. Wells' noticing. The cops don't have a big interest in finding her. Except — I can't remember if I mentioned it before — Brandon did slip her a note on the back of his business card before she left. But that's just another 'so what,' as far as the cops are concerned. And that's about everything I know, for now. You feel okay as far as the Hawkins job?"

"Yeah. If you follow my paper trail, I never left the States."

"How did you get there?"

"Sailboat. It was a throwaway. I sunk it on the way back, somewhere out in the Gulf Stream. Some guy I never heard of bought it from a private seller, never re-registered it. Cleared in at Bimini with fake ship's papers. That's the end of his trail, if anybody ever finds the beginning."

"Cool. So what are you two up to now?"

"We're chilling out, for now," Mary said. "Waiting to see what happens next."

"Why don't you take a road trip?" Aaron said. "Drive up the coast. Take your time. Plan on spending a few days in Savannah and Charleston. That's pretty country."

"What would people like us find to amuse ourselves in Savannah? Or Charleston?" I asked.

"Oh, you'll find something in one or the other. Stay in touch; I'll do a little checking. By the time you get to Savannah, I should have some ideas for you."

"We'll do that, Aaron," I said. "You've never steered me wrong yet."

"Stay safe, you two."

"Thanks, Aaron." I disconnected the call and looked at Mary.

"Are you as sleepy as I am?" she asked.

"At least," I said. "What say we take a nice, long nap? If we wake up before nightfall, maybe we can check out and drive for a few hours."

"That sounds good, but I should check out of my room next door first. That way, if anybody checks, they won't find two people in adjoining rooms who left together."

"Okay," I said.

Mary went through the connecting door and came back with a good-sized backpack. She dropped it in the corner of my room.

"You going down to the desk?" I asked.

She shook her head. "I prepaid. I'll just call the desk and leave my key in the room, but there's a voicemail on the room phone."

"Who's it from?"

"I don't know. Probably a wrong number. Nobody knows I was even here, let alone what name I used. I'll be right back."

In a few seconds, she called out to me. "Hey, Finn?"

"Yes?"

"Come here and listen to this before I erase it."

I went through the door and found her with the receiver in one hand and her iPhone in the other. She held the iPhone close to the earpiece of the room phone, and I could hear the message although not well enough to understand it. In a few seconds, she thumbed the screen of the iPhone and stuck it in her pocket.

Handing me the receiver, she said, "I'll play it for you. While you listen, I want to make sure I got a good recording of it. Then we can erase it."

"Okay," I said, holding the receiver to my ear.

She pressed a key on the room phone and then stepped away, taking her iPhone from her pocket.

I listened, not sure what to expect.

"Hello, Ms. Maloney. You don't know me yet, but I've been keeping track of your recent workings.

You impressed me; I could use someone with your skills in my business. Vasily Zaytsev — you should be checking on the web. You will perhaps see what I mean. You work briefly for the man I acquired my U.S. operations from, if that maybe help you to understand what I mean.

I will arrange to have two of my men pick you up and bring you to meet me. I do not wish to alarm you, so I tell you in advance that they will blindfold you before they bring you to me. Believe me when I say I wish you no harm. This is merely the precaution to protect both of us, so do not worry.

I know your skills, so I wish for you to consent in advance, so there will be no difficulty with my men. Please to respond by text to 912 321 1550 with the word "okay," and we will take matters in hand. Please not to call that number, as will not be answered.

   Thank you in advance. I look forward to do business with you."

"The Russian," I said.

"That's my bet," Mary said. "The blindfold business matches what I heard about him after we took care of Senator Lee. What do you think I should do?"

"Did you catch the time of the message?"

"Yes. It came in at 1:30 this morning," she said.

"I heard the Eastern European accent. Did you?"

"I heard an accent," Mary said. "I don't have enough experience to place it, though."

"How's the recording you made?"

"Good enough," she said. "What do you think we should do?"

"Let's erase the voicemail, and you should check out of this room. He can't be sure you got the message until you respond."

"You think I should?" she asked. "Respond, I mean?"

"Not just yet. We'll do a little checking first. Go ahead. Call the desk and tell them you're leaving."

"I'm not sure we should stay here, Finn. Not even just for a few more hours."

"I agree. But let's take it a step at a time. You check out. Then we'll figure out how to get out of here without their spotting us."

"You think they're watching me?"

"Yes."

"Yeah, I do, too. I'm spooked."

"We're okay. Stay cool. They won't jump you just yet. I would take your friend Vasily at his word, for the moment. He's tipped you off for a reason."

"He doesn't want me to kill the men he sends? That's what you're saying?"

"Yes. He doesn't want to kill you, either. At least not yet. He may want to hire you. Or maybe interrogate you. Check out and leave. I'll be a few minutes behind you. We'll meet at the airport. Then we'll send the recording to Aaron and let him work his magic while we figure out how to deal with this."

"Okay. But where are we going?"

"Driving to Savannah, like Aaron suggested."

"Aha!" she said, grinning. "Got it."

Mary picked up the phone and called the desk. "I'm checking out of my room," she said. "I'll leave the key on the dresser, okay?"

She nodded and hung up the phone.

"Okay," I said. "I'm going back to my room. I'll hand you your backpack and we'll lock the connecting doors. You leave from your room's main door. Get a cab to the airport. Buy yourself a ticket to somewhere on a flight that's leaving soon. Go through security and get yourself a cup of coffee. Kill a half hour and then head for baggage claim. I'll pick you up curbside at the Concourse D arrivals area. Call me about five minutes before you step outside; I'll be in the car in the cellphone waiting lane."

She nodded and gave me a quick kiss. "See you soon, sailor."

I gave her a hug and handed her the backpack. She closed the connecting door, and I packed up my few belongings.

14

I GAVE MARY A 45-MINUTE HEAD-START AND THEN GOT IN MY
rental car. It was a 15-minute drive to the airport. I would call the
hotel once I got there and let them know I wouldn't be back; they
could charge the room to my credit card.

As I settled into the rhythm of the traffic, I let my thoughts
wander back over what we knew about the Russian. Several
weeks ago, Mary and I dispatched the crooked senator, Jefferson
Davis Lee, at his house in a gated golf community nearby. He was
a high-profile target, and only a few days before we hit him, Mary
and I killed a crooked FBI agent in St. Thomas.

We split up, not wanting to press our luck. Lee and the FBI
agent were part of the same criminal enterprise. The tie between
our victims might enable our opponents to guess that we were
working together. To make our connection less obvious, I flew
back to the British Virgin Islands; Mary stayed behind in south
Florida to do a little research.

We suspected that someone would try to take over the
O'Hanlon mob after Rory O'Hanlon's death. Mary asked around,
using connections from her time as a freelance contract
killer. She learned that there was a mysterious, shadowy char-

acter who was making the rounds of O'Hanlon's former lieutenants.

His identity eluded her sources. No one even knew what he looked like. He would arrange for two of his troops to pick up a potential recruit and bring the candidate to meet him. The candidate was blindfolded for the round trip and the meeting.

Mary gleaned two other pieces of information. One was that the mystery man spoke with a slight accent, perhaps Eastern European. The other was more ominous.

One interviewee arranged for his own people to follow him after he was picked up. The mystery man's people lost the tail, and the meeting was uneventful. The candidate thought he secured a good deal with his new master. A few days later, he was found in his office, dead. Every bone in his body was broken. This was a trademark of the Russian Mafia; the mode of death is called *zamochit*. The mystery man valued his anonymity.

Back then, Mary and I were still planning to kill my former boss's boss, who was also involved in the kidnapping of my daughter. He, too, was found in his home office, every bone broken. The mystery man got to him before we did, but we didn't know why. Was the Russian worried that he knew too much?

I had passed the information along to Aaron Sanchez, hoping he could learn more about the mysterious Russian. That was when Aaron discovered the two DoJ investigations.

Aaron also learned that the DoJ suspected there might be several Russians involved, not just one. There were indications that the Russians were agents of their government as opposed to being gangsters, although it could be hard to tell the difference. Vasily Zaytsev might as well have introduced himself as the Russian mystery man in the voicemail he left Mary.

At the airport, I pulled into the waiting area close to Concourse D arrivals. Almost an hour had passed since Mary left the hotel. Minutes after I set the parking brake, Mary called.

"I'll be out at the curb in a couple of minutes," she said.

"See you then." I pulled out of the waiting area.

I PULLED to the curb in the arrivals area, and an unfamiliar woman in a business suit approached the car. She opened the back door and tossed in a duffle bag. Closing the door, she got into the front passenger seat. The auburn wig and the suit made a big difference in Mary's appearance.

"You look like the woman who killed Brandon," I said, as she fastened her seatbelt.

"My choices were limited," she said. "I thought a change of appearance was in order, though."

"Where did you get the disguise?"

"My backpack. I still had the clothes and the wig from the other night. But you're the only one who saw me dressed this way."

"Where's the backpack?" I asked, pulling out into traffic.

"In the duffle bag, and the duffle bag was rolled up in the backpack before I changed. A girl never knows when she might need to dress up."

"Good for you. If they're watching me or the car, this should throw them off."

"You think they're watching you?"

"I haven't spotted anybody, but you never know. I thought we could get on the road and switch cars along the way."

"Okay," she said. "While I was killing time in the gate area, I went online and searched for Vasily Zaytsev."

"And what did you learn?"

"He was a famous Russian sniper in World War II, a Hero of the Soviet Union. Literally hundreds of kills to his credit. He died in 1991."

"Interesting. I wonder why our mystery man sent you looking for him. Think he's sending you a message of some kind?"

She shrugged. "If he is, it's lost on me. Should we call Aaron?"

"Sure. Get him on the horn."

She took her Phorcys-provided phone from her purse and placed the call.

"Mary?"

"Hi, Aaron. You're on the speaker," she said. "We're both here."

"Okay. What's new with you two?"

"We're on the Interstate headed north," I said. "We'll need a little logistics help, but first, Mary has a new admirer."

"Oh? Who's that?" Aaron asked.

Mary told him about the voicemail and about her internet research. "When we hang up," she said, "I'll email a recording of the voicemail to you."

"Have you responded to him?" Aaron asked.

"No. We figure he was having me watched; we wanted to lose the tail first. Plus, we haven't come up with a plan for responding."

"You don't think they're following you now?" he asked.

I told Aaron about Mary's false trail. "Mary's probably clean now, but it's possible they're following me. I haven't spotted a tail yet, but who knows? That brings us to the logistics help I mentioned."

"Okay," Aaron said. "What do you need?"

"Fresh identities and a rental car to match. We'll pick them up at the Orlando airport this evening."

"Not a problem. Here's what I recommend. Turn in your car there and take the shuttle to the terminal. Split up. Get tickets to anywhere with your current IDs, and go through security. Then head for the shuttles and go to the hotel in the airport complex. The concierge desk will have a package for Jerome Finnegan. That will have your new identities. There will be a car reserved in Finn's new name. Or Mary's. Your choice — just pick one now. Details will be in the package."

"Use Finn," Mary said. "They found me at the hotel where I

was using the Maloney name. They may not have a name for Finn, if they even connected us."

"Good enough. Should I book a room there in your new name, while I'm at it?"

"No, thanks," I said. "We'll stop somewhere else around there for the night, but we should get clear of the airport as quickly as we can, just in case."

"Okay. Anything else I can do for you now?"

"I think that's it," I said.

"Drive safely. I'll be in touch as soon as I find out anything on the Russian."

"Thanks, Aaron," Mary said.

"You're welcome. Talk with you later."

Mary disconnected the call and put the phone away.

"Any ideas on how I should respond to my pal Vasily?"

"Some, but we should wait until we get to the airport in Orlando, for sure. We can get throwaway phones to use. They'll try to track down the phone you use to send the text."

"Yeah, no doubt. I was thinking a step or two beyond that, though. Think we can turn this around on him?"

"Maybe," I said. "But we might want to string him along for a while, depending on whether Aaron's able to learn anything."

"Seems to me there's not much hope of that," Mary said. "You know that phone number he left will be a burner."

"Probably. But there's a chance he didn't call from that number."

"How would Aaron know that? There was no caller ID on the room phone."

"Aaron's got somebody who can hack into the hotel's phone system. They might get a real phone number for Vasily. Depends on how careful he was. How are you thinking we could turn this around on him, anyway?"

"My first thought is to snatch the two guys he sends to pick me up. No telling what we might learn from them. The other option's for me to go through with the meeting and see what happens."

"I don't like that one," I said.

"You could follow us when his guys pick me up."

"That plan didn't work so well for the last person who tried it."

"Yeah, but we know that. We can learn from his mistake. Once I'm face to face with Vasily, I could take him down."

"That's risky, Mary. I know you're good, but this guy's no amateur, and he'll have backup. At least the two men who pick you up. Probably more troops, too."

"They won't be scared of me. I'm just another woman, as far as they're concerned. That's my edge, Finn. It works every time."

"Except that he's already seen you at work. Or at least, he's seen the results. You can't bank on him underestimating you. I know what you're saying — no matter how much they know, when they see you, they still think you're a helpless female. But Vasily's not your average badass."

"You think I'm too cocky?"

"I don't think anything. I just want overwhelming odds in our favor. We won't get those by playing his game, or even a variation of it. Let it rest for a while. You'll come up with something. Time is on our side but as soon as you respond, the clock starts running. We need as much information as we can get before that happens."

"I see what you mean. I'm just worried that if I don't respond, he'll escalate things, maybe come after me."

"That's actually the option I was considering," I said. "That might give us the advantage. Think about it."

"I will. How long before we get to Orlando? Three hours?"

"Give or take, yeah. Why?"

"I'm thinking about a nap," she said.

"Go for it."

"Promise to wake me in an hour and a half?" Mary asked. "Then I'll drive and you can get a little rest."

"You've got a deal."

15

"You feel up to calling Aaron?" I asked. "Let's see if he's got anything new on the Russian."

Mary and I were settled for the night in an inexpensive motel. We checked in under our new identities, thanks to Aaron and his support people.

"Sure," Mary said. "Call him."

I took my encrypted phone from my pocket and placed the call.

"Good evening, Finn. Did everything come out okay in Orlando?"

"Yes, thanks. We're in good shape. We've stopped for the night; I'm not sure exactly where we are — some exit off I-95 north of Titusville. Any news on the Russian?"

"Yeah, as a matter of fact. I was about to call you, but we weren't quite ready yet."

"We?" Mary asked.

"Hi, Mary," Aaron said. "Yeah. Mike wanted to talk with you. He and Bob have been kicking things around since I passed along that recording you sent."

"Oh," I said. "What's on their minds?"

"I'm not sure, but we're about to find out. Mike's on the other line. Hang on."

We were on hold for 15 seconds, then Aaron came back on the line.

"Mary? Finn?"

"Yes," Mary said. "We're here."

"Good evening," Mike Killington said.

"Evening, Mike," Mary said.

"Hi, Mike. What's up?" I asked.

"Several of us have been discussing Mary's voicemail. Aaron's been busy with his hackers, too, trying to correlate other intel with that call. He can fill you in on that in a minute. First, though, we've revised our plans. This Russian thing looks like an opportunity we shouldn't pass up. We've put the actions in Savannah and Charleston on hold, for now. I don't think you've gotten past the point of no return on those, have you?"

Aaron said, "Sir, if I may..."

"Yes, Aaron?"

"Bob called me with the target information for Savannah, but when I told him about the voicemail, he said I should hold off calling Finn and Mary."

"Ah," Mike said. "Okay, then. Good. We'll get back to that, but we want to go after this Russian character first. Everybody on board with that? Any problems you see with it?"

Mary looked at me and raised her eyebrows, motioning for me to talk. "No problem with the shift in priorities," I said. "Does this mean you want him terminated?"

"Well, that's why I wanted to talk with the three of you. Aaron's told you that the DoJ was investigating this character, I believe?"

"Yes," I said.

"And there was a connection between the Russian and this political consultant, Rayburn. Right?"

"Right. He told us Rayburn was working as an informant for

the DoJ's investigation into the Russian, but that's as far as we got."

"That's all there is, except the DoJ's in a tizzy about Rayburn and his undercover protective detail. They aren't buying the story the police have come up with. Aaron's team has picked up confusing signals related to the DoJ's investigation, too. He can tell you about those later, but we suspect they weren't trying to build a case against O'Hanlon or the Russian."

"Then why the investigation?" Mary asked.

"We can only guess, but we suspect it was a smokescreen. They could keep anybody else from poking their nose into the situation by claiming they were already there. Anybody else might jeopardize their investigation."

"Mary and I were wondering if the DoJ was part of a coverup," I said, "given how deeply the corruption seems to go."

"That's a good possibility, which brings us to the Russian. I know this is a little different for you, Finn, but we'd prefer to infiltrate the Russian's operation instead of executing him. There's a whole layer of corruption that's not reflected in the files we got from O'Hanlon. That's where Rayburn fit in. What's your reaction?"

"To spying on the Russian?" I asked.

"Yes. He's opened that possibility with Mary."

"Unless he just wants to kill her," I said.

"Why go to all that trouble?" Mary asked. "He knew where I was staying. He left the voicemail on my room phone, so he could have sent his troops after me if he wanted me dead."

"Unless he wants something else from you," I said.

"Like what?" she asked. "The files are already in the open, so to speak."

"Yes," Mike said. "But you raise a good point, between the two of you. We have the files, and the Russian is watching as we pick off the people listed in them. But he's trying to take over O'Hanlon's operation. Having his own copy of the files would make it a lot easier for him."

"I thought he was working with O'Hanlon," Mary said. "So wouldn't he already have the information?"

"Maybe," Mike said. "Or maybe not. O'Hanlon was a cagey man; those files were the keys to his kingdom. Giving the Russian access to selected people would have been a lot different from giving him the whole roster."

"Why would he do that, though? O'Hanlon, I mean?"

"We don't know, but it's clear that the Russian is working his way through O'Hanlon's lieutenants one step at a time. Maybe every time he recruits a new person, he gets a list of who they know. There's a reason he's moving so slowly. That could be why."

"We could feed him an edited list," I said.

"Yes, maybe so. But first we have to contact him. How do you feel about that, Mary? Are you willing to meet with him?"

Mary motioned for me to be quiet. "Yes, but I think I need to play hard to get. Finn and I were talking about why Vasily wants me to agree to the meeting before he sends his people to pick me up."

"You know his name's not really Vasily Zaytsev," Aaron said. "Vasily Zaytsev was — "

"A Russian sniper in World War II," Mary interrupted. "It's just easier to call him Vasily than 'the Russian.'"

"What do you make of his approach, Mary?" Mike said.

"I'm taking it at face value. As Finn said, Vasily's seen me at work. He knows if his men try to pick me up against my will, somebody might die. It could be me, or it could be them. Either way, unless he's planning to kill me, that result wouldn't be attractive to him. So I don't think he wants to kill me, at least not yet."

"That makes sense. So do you think you should meet with him?"

"I think I should respond, but with caution. I'm thinking in terms of a counter offer."

"What kind of counter offer?"

"A meeting on neutral ground, somewhere public, where neither of us would have a particular advantage. He said he didn't mean me harm, so it's reasonable for me to make him prove it. If both sides knew in advance where the meeting was going to be, we could each have protection in place, at a distance. I would even propose that to him."

"What type of protection?" Mike asked.

"My pick would be Finn with a sniper rifle on a rooftop. I would tell Vasily that I was protected and if I gave the signal, he would be shot dead on the spot. I would encourage him to arrange the same for me. Like the old Cold War strategy of mutually assured destruction. We both walk away, or neither of us walks away."

"There's a big problem with that," I said.

"What's that?" Mary asked, frowning at me.

"We don't know what he looks like. He could send somebody else. But we believe he does know what you look like."

"That's not the point, Finn. It's a credible counteroffer, that's all. We don't have to go through with it. I don't want to start out by accepting his terms."

"As long as you don't go through with it, maybe. But if you don't follow through on the meeting, you're inviting him to blow you away."

"But we already established that if he wanted to do that, he wouldn't go about it by setting up a meeting," Mary said. "He wants something, like the files. He might try to kill me after he gets them. Or he may want to recruit me as his enforcer; that's the way I read the voicemail. Either way, I figure he will want me to walk away from that first meeting. Then we can argue about the next step. Mike? Aaron? Any thoughts?"

"All those ideas are worth thinking about," Mike said. "Let them rest for a few minutes, and Aaron can tell us what his people have learned since you sent us that recording earlier. Okay?"

"Sure," Mary said.

"Okay with me," I said.

"Aaron?" Mike asked.

"All right. First, the number he gave you in the voicemail is a prepaid cellphone. We haven't been able to figure out where it was purchased, but it has been on the network off and on in the Miami area since about midnight last night. That would be a little before the voicemail was left on your room phone, Mary. Is that right?"

"Yes. The time on the message was 1:30 a.m."

"Right," Aaron said. "That prepaid phone placed a call to a local number in Miami at about 12:30 a.m., and a few minutes later, it got a call-back from the same number. Following me?"

"Yes," Mary said. "Did you get the local number?"

"We did. I'll get to that. We also hacked the phone system at your hotel. The voicemail came from a third number, but the caller ID was spoofed, to cover their tracks. We managed to back-track it, though. It was the same local number in Miami. It's a phone in a hotel business service lounge. That's also where the prepaid cellphone was when those two calls were made. They were probably just testing it, maybe testing their spoofing, too."

"Dead end, then?" I asked.

"Probably, but we don't know. We have the hotel's security videos; we're checking them as we speak, but they aren't the best quality. We'll see. We also have taps on the personal and office phones of the people at the DoJ who were working Rayburn. We just got those in place earlier today. There's a lot of traffic to get through; the only real intelligence we got is that they've lost contact with the Russian. They used Rayburn and one of the marshals to communicate with him. So they're working madly to set up a new channel to Vasily, but it's not going smoothly so far. And that's about all I have for now."

"It's going on 20 hours since he left me that voicemail," Mary said. "What do you think about responding? I'm worried that if I don't respond at all, he'll escalate."

"He might try," Mike said. "But you've laid a pretty good false trail. Aaron told me about your evasion. Unless they followed you through both airports, they won't know where you are. But you do have a valid point. Do you have any particular response in mind?"

"Something brief and not informative," Mary said. "How about, 'Interested in meeting you. Traveling now. Back in Miami in a few days. Contact you then.'"

"I can't see the harm in that," Mike said. "It might buy us a little time. What do you think, Aaron?"

"If nothing else, it will give us a shot at getting another location for that prepaid cellphone he's using."

"Good point," Mike said. "Finn?"

"Sounds okay to me."

"Good. Mary, send your text to Aaron on your secure phone when we hang up. Aaron, you send the text from an untraceable number that appears to be in another state. If you can get a location for the burner phone that the Russian is using, scramble a team to see who's in the area, but no contact, okay?"

"Okay."

"Good. We'll talk again at 7:00 a.m. unless something comes up sooner. Goodnight, everybody."

"Goodnight," Mary and I said. I disconnected the call.

"Ready to sack out?" Mary asked, yawning, as she sent her text to Aaron.

"I'm beyond ready," I said.

16

HAVING TURNED IN EARLY LAST NIGHT, MARY AND I WENT TO breakfast and returned to our room before our 7:00 a.m. conference call. We were sipping from large cups of takeout coffee when my encrypted phone rang.

"Hello, Aaron, Mike," I said, answering it.

"Good morning, Finn," Aaron said. "Is Mary with you?"

"Yes, I'm here," she said. "Good morning."

"Good morning to both of you," Mike said. "Aaron's team was busy last night. Aaron, why don't you start things off?"

"All right. We sent that message you composed, Mary. The phone that received it was on a motor yacht at one of the big marinas in Fort Lauderdale. *Anastasia* is her name. Her hailing port's Georgetown, Cayman Islands. You know what that means, right?"

Mary shook her head, looking at me.

"Owned by some brass-plate corporation?" I asked.

"Yeah, exactly. We're working to find out who's behind the shell company, but don't hold your breath. We have the vessel under surveillance, though. I take it the name means nothing to either of you."

"Not to me," Mary said.

"Nor to me," I said. "Was there any reaction to the message?"

"There hasn't been a reply yet, but yeah, there was a reaction, all right," Aaron said, chuckling. "We sent Mary's text from a burner phone after we spoke last night. We left the phone in a motel room just south of Savannah. The room is in the name Mary Helen Maloney, to match the name he used for you in the voice mail, Mary. About two hours after we sent the text, two men picked the lock on the door and tossed the room."

"Two hours, huh? Quick response," I said.

"Yeah. They're from Savannah," Aaron said. "Not a big surprise that he has troops there. That's one of the places where he met with O'Hanlon's people, from what Mary picked up earlier. Good chance they're working for the man who was going to be your next target, before the Russian reared his head."

"Was anything in the room for them to find besides the phone?" Mary asked.

"The bed was slept in, and there was some luggage, but that's it. The car listed on your room registration wasn't in the parking lot. We don't know for sure if they checked for the car, but they probably did. They were thorough. After their search, they put the room back the way they found it and set up surveillance outside the motel."

"You still have a team in place, then?" I asked. "Watching the watchers?"

"Yes, for now. And that's everything, so far."

"Thanks, Aaron," Mike said. "Good work. We need to figure out where we go from here. Any ideas, anybody?"

"What about that car?" Mary asked. "You said the license plate number was on the room registration?"

"Yes. It's a rental, in the Maloney name. They'll probably know that by now. We have the car, still, pending our decision as to what's next. But it's not where they'll find it."

"Let's do a quick list of options from here," I suggested.

"Sure," Mike said. "Lead the way, Finn. I'll make notes."

"Okay. Here goes:

"One: Pick up the two men who're watching the hotel and interrogate them.

"Two: Use the car to lay a false trail to lead them to somewhere of our choosing.

"Three: Send in a decoy who can pass for Mary and see what they do when she goes into the room.

"Nothing else comes to mind just yet."

"What about that cellphone?" Mary asked. "The one in the room?"

"It's there, turned on, plugged into the charger," Aaron said. "Why do you ask?"

"Because that's the only contact number he has for me, as far as we know. If he sends a text or leaves a voicemail on it, we won't know."

"Good for you, Mary," Aaron said. "But thanks to the miracles of modern technology, we *will* know. We're able to monitor that phone remotely. We can even make calls or send texts that will appear to come from it."

"Okay. I was wondering about that. Then here's my idea. Let's send him another text from that phone. I'll point out to him that by sending those men, he's proven I can't trust him. I'll tell him I'm still interested in doing business with him, but I'm not willing to meet with him."

"We can do that," Aaron said, "But his two men are watching the room. They'll tell him there was nobody in there to send the message."

"Yes, I know," Mary said. "There are two ways to deal with that. I'm not sure which one I like better."

"Let's hear them," Mike said.

"First option, we kill his surveillance team."

Mike laughed at that. "I like your style; it must be in your genes. That was Bob's idea, as well. Before we explore that one, what's your other option?"

"Send the message anyway and let him wonder how I did it. It tells him something about the technical resources at my disposal."

"Any other ideas? Finn? Aaron?"

"Not as far as the motel goes," I said. "I have a few ideas about the motor yacht, but let's work through Mary's two first."

"Yeah, I'm for that, too," Aaron said.

"Mary?" Mike asked.

"Yes?"

"Give us the pros and cons of killing the surveillance team."

"It doesn't raise the question of how we manipulated the telephone network. It's the kind of thing he might do if the situation were reversed, so it reinforces his appreciation for my skills, maybe piques his interest. It doesn't give him the idea that there's a big, technically savvy organization behind me — just makes me look better at the game than his own people. Those are all consistent with why he *said* he wanted to do business with me."

"Good," Mike said. "What about the cons?"

"Two dead men, maybe for no real reason."

"Does that bother you?" Mike asked.

"No. They took that risk when they came after me. But it's a complication. There will be the problem of the bodies — whether to leave them as a message or make them disappear, say in the Okefenokee Swamp. It's close by there. And we risk escalating things. Maybe he was just flexing his muscle. He may have sent them to pick me up, even though I wanted to delay meeting him — just to set the tone of our relationship going forward. To show me who was the boss. If that's the case, he'll almost have to bump the violence up a notch. He's not likely to let a woman have the upper hand for long."

"Anything to add?" Mike asked, after a few seconds of silence.

"No," I said, and Aaron echoed that.

"Tell us more about your second option, Mary," Mike said.

"Okay. If we send the message from the phone and his people know there was nobody in the room, he learns something new about me. That could be good or bad, depending on how we play it and what he really wants from me.

"So far, he thinks I killed the Daileys and stole the records and the money they managed for O'Hanlon. He would have learned that from O'Hanlon. Most likely, he suspects I killed O'Hanlon and his people in Martinique.

"He may or may not know I was part of taking out George Kelley and his thugs in St. Thomas. Ditto for the hit on Senator Lee, and Nora Lewis, or whoever he thought she was."

"But all that happened a while back," Mike said. "Why did he wait so long to call you?"

"Uh... Maybe it took him that long to find me?"

I hit the mute button on the phone. "I think you should come clean with him, Mary. He may know anyway, and he won't pry into why you went walkabout. Bob's fixed that for you."

She scrunched up her face for a second and nodded, touching the mute button. "Sorry for the delay; I was thinking."

"No problem," Mike said. "Thinking's good. Any ideas?"

"Yes. About that personal business I took care of in the last week or so..."

"You think it's related?" Mike asked.

"Well, as Finn is fond of saying, it's hard to overlook coincidence. I took the time off to nail two personal targets, but I had no idea they were part of this. They were people who — "

I put my hand on her arm and leaned toward her, whispering in her ear. "Skip the explanation. Cut to the chase."

She looked at me and nodded. "Sorry. I was wandering. What you need to know is that I killed Louie Rayburn. Louie may have told the Russian about me after he took me in."

"Aha!" Aaron said. "You were the girl in the 'skirt slit up to here?' The one the Wells woman claimed to have seen."

"Yes," Mary said. "And that business card that Brandon slipped me in the Pink Parrot that night? It had a note on it asking me to come to his office at 5:30 the next evening."

"And?"

"And I did. He let me in without anybody knowing, and I killed him. There was a lot of coincidence between those two hits. My bet is that's what brought me to the Russian's attention."

"Okay," Mike said. "That fits; once he identified you and knew you were in Miami, it wasn't too hard for him to find you. That's a good explanation for the timing, anyhow."

"Right," Mary said. "The Russian already knew *what* I was from O'Hanlon, but after Rayburn and Brandon, he knew *who* I was. Or so he thinks. This is all useful background, but unless you have more questions, I'll get back to my point about sending him another text about his two goons."

"Yes," Mike said. "Thanks for the fill-in, but please do go ahead with your second idea."

"All right. If he gets a text from that phone and he knows it's in an empty motel room, he'll know that I'm not just a garden-variety contract killer. I — "

Mike's laughter interrupted Mary. "Sorry," he said, "but the notion of you as a 'garden-variety contract killer' just hit my funny bone. Please, go ahead."

Mary smiled. "Okay. What I was trying to say is that he won't be expecting that kind of technical capability from somebody he thinks is just a hired gun. It might make him suspect I'm working for a government agency."

"But he has the government in his pocket," Aaron said. "Or he thinks he does, anyway."

"Our government, yes," Mike said. "There are other governments that might be after this character, for all we know. He may have worked in other places besides the U.S. But Mary makes a good point. If we send him a text from that phone when he knows there's nobody around it, it will put her in a different league in his eyes. As it stands now, he might underestimate what he's up against. If we send that message, he'll be on full alert. Finn, you've been quiet. What do you think?"

"We're overthinking this," I said. "Let's say Mary sent that first message and left the phone in her room. Then she went out for a drive. What would happen when she came back and discovered someone broke into her room?"

"But wait," Mary said. "They're watching the hotel, waiting for me to come back. They know I haven't returned."

"No," I said. "They know they didn't *see* you return. Suppose you were covering your tracks and you ditched the car? You could sneak back into the hotel without them seeing you. You would check the door to your room for intrusion. You could have left a tiny length of thread, or a feather, or something they dislodged when they broke in."

"Oh, right," Mary said. "We've both done that kind of thing. So if I spotted that, I might not go into the room. It could be booby trapped, or they could be waiting in there."

"Exactly," I said. "Then what would you do?"

"Get the hell out of Dodge?" she asked. "That's what you're thinking?"

"Yes. And what about responding to his message?"

"How do I know about it?" she asked.

"You checked for text messages to that phone number with another device, maybe. Or maybe you were there when the message came in and that's why you split. You left the phone because you figured they were tracking it once you sent them the text."

"Then I would respond from another burner phone, right? I have his number; I don't need to use that phone in the room."

"Bingo! Like I said, we were overthinking the situation."

"That opens a range of new options," Mike said. "Thanks, Finn. What else can you add?"

"I think Aaron should send a response on Mary's behalf. Say

something like she suggested — 'Now that I know I can't trust you, I'm not willing to meet, but I'm still interested in doing business. For now, though, I'm busy with a job for somebody else. If you make me a better offer, I could drop this deal — but it will cost you.'

"It should come from a burner phone somewhere that we've staked out, just to see if he scrambles a team to find it. Kind of like recon by fire. We'll see how he reacts and go from there. Meanwhile, he thinks she's still in the Savannah area. He will warn the target there, if he hasn't already. That means we should hit somebody else the Russian has recruited. Maybe Charleston?"

Mary laughed. "You're going to make him paranoid."

"Maybe," I said. "We could use you like one of Medusa's sisters."

"Medusa's sisters?" Mary asked.

"The Sirens," I said. "Well, maybe the Sirens weren't exactly her sisters, but the Romans thought Phorcys was their father and Medusa's, so they were related."

"What are you talking about, Finn?" she asked.

"The Odyssey. If you sing your siren song sweetly enough, you can lure the Russian and his motor yacht onto the rocks, at least figuratively."

"I like it, Finn," Mike said. "Let's make it happen. Aaron, you know what to do. Mary, you and Finn head for Charleston. That's an easy drive from where you are, right?"

"Five or six hours, depending on traffic," Mary said. "Should we leave now?"

"You may as well. Get yourselves situated there. We'll queue things up and touch base this evening for the target briefing. Anything else we need to cover now?"

I looked at Mary and raised my eyebrows. She shook her head.

"Not from our end," I said.

"We'll talk to you this evening," Mary said.

"Good," Mike said. "You two drive safely. Aaron, stay on the line, please."

There was a click as the connection dropped. Mary smiled at me.

"So I'm a siren, now? Luring sailors onto the rocks?"

I nodded. "It worked with me; the Russian doesn't stand a chance. Let's hit the road, siren."

17

"WHAT'S ON YOUR MIND?" I ASKED.

She looked over at me and smiled. "Thinking about Mike's reaction to my confession about Rayburn and Brandon."

"What reaction?"

"That's what I mean. He didn't have much of a reaction. Do you think he knew already? You didn't tell him, did you?"

"I told you I wouldn't, Mary. That was your story to tell, or not. But I thought it would be best for you to tell him just now."

"I agree; I'm glad you suggested it. But he didn't seem surprised."

"No. But guys like Mike guard their reactions. You'll never know what he's thinking, unless he wants you to."

"I think he knew. Or at least suspected. How could he have found out?"

I shrugged. "You didn't give Bob Lawson any details?"

"None. Just that there were two men I needed to settle up with for my mother."

"Well," I said, "there are two things that could have tipped Bob and Mike off. One is my old friend, coincidence. They knew you were on the loose and that you started out when you got to Miami. Five people were killed in Miami in ways that misled the cops. That points to you, or somebody like you. And they know I didn't do it."

"Okay. That's one thing. You said there were two. What's the other thing?"

"Your Uncle Bob may know more about your mother's life than you think."

Mary frowned and didn't say anything for 30 seconds. Then she asked, "Why do you say that, Finn?"

"It wouldn't be surprising. He was her older brother, and you said he tried to help her from time to time."

"Half-assed attempts," she said, frowning again.

"You were 12 when she died, right?"

"Yes. So?"

"Her life was a wreck for as long as you can remember; you've told me that. Isn't it possible that Bob tried to intervene, maybe before you were old enough to know what was going on?"

"I suppose. But when she died, where was he? When I was caught up in the foster care system?"

"You told me he was in the Middle East when she died, Mary. And that he hired private detectives to try to find you."

"Yes. You're right. He did. I thought I was past being angry about that, but..."

"I understand. The reason I even brought it up is that there's every reason to believe that he might have discovered her connection to Rayburn and Brandon. It could have surfaced when he was looking for you, or even before she died, you know?"

"I never thought of that," Mary said. "But why didn't he do something about them earlier?"

"There could be any number of reasons. If you want to know, you'll have to ask him. But it wouldn't be surprising if he guessed which two men from your mother's past you were going after, would it?"

"No, it wouldn't. You're right. So there's a good chance Mike already knew I killed them. Did you figure that out earlier? I mean, is that why you encouraged me to come clean with Mike on the call this morning?"

"Yes. Like I said, Mike and Bob aren't the kind of people you want to mislead. Not when they're on your side."

She was silent for a few seconds, and then she looked over at me and said, "Thanks, Finn."

"You're welcome, but you would have gotten there on your own."

"That's not why I said thanks. You had it all figured out, but you let me save face. You're a good, kind, thoughtful man."

I chuckled.

"Why are you laughing?"

"Because most people would think I'm a monster, given my history. I don't know that anybody's ever said I was good and kind and thoughtful."

"Most people don't know you the way I do," she said.

"Well, anyway, I'm glad you like me. I wouldn't want you for an enemy, Miss Garden-Variety Killer."

"Speaking of that, do you know who we're going after in Charleston?" Mary asked.

"No. I thought you might have a clue."

"Not me. All I picked up was that it was somebody in the shipping industry."

"That makes sense," I said. "Charleston's a big port; probably a good place to bring in contraband."

"Yeah. I like Charleston and Savannah. They're pretty places, and there are lots of good places to eat."

I laughed.

"Why are you laughing, Finn?"

"I don't think of you as being fond of good places to eat; your tastes are like mine — food's fuel."

"You're right. But I'm running close to empty; how about stopping for lunch?"

"All right. We're approaching St. Augustine; there's bound to be somewhere."

She rummaged in her duffle bag and took out her iPhone, opening the web browser. "I'll find a place. Seafood okay?"

"Yes, ma'am. Sounds good to me."

MARY and I were relaxing in our room, waiting for Aaron's call. She found a bed-and-breakfast near Charleston's Battery; we were pretending to be tourists for cover. We planned to have a late dinner at a place within walking distance after Aaron's call. At 7 o'clock, my encrypted phone rang.

"Hi, Aaron," I said, taking the call in speaker mode.

"Hi, yourself. Mary with you?"

"Yes, I'm here. Good evening Aaron."

"Hi. Are you two in Charleston?"

"Yes. All set to be tourists. Is Mike going to join us?" I asked.

"No. Not unless you need him for something. We figured this call would be straightforward enough. Before we get to the mission, though, let me tell you about that motel outside Savannah; you'll get a kick out of what happened."

"What happened?" Mary asked.

"Well, the first thing we discovered is that we underestimated their surveillance. They had four people, not two. There were the two outside I mentioned before, but they also had a man and woman in a room across the hall. We aren't sure when they moved them in, yet, but we'll find out later this evening. Anyhow, they're all gone now, back to Savannah. It's only a few minutes away.

"The maid showed up to clean Mary's room at 11:30 — checkout time was 11:00. She found the room unoccupied, with all the stuff we left there. Her supervisor called the manager, who called the phone number on the registration. That was the burner that was in the room, and it didn't take them long to figure that out. The manager told the maid to pack up the stuff and move it to their lost-and-found room. We paid cash in advance and they didn't have a credit card they could charge for another night. Plus, they were overbooked this evening, so they needed the room. This was all as we planned, but then it got amusing.

"The watchers in the room across the hall saw what was happening, and the man went down to the desk and asked the manager what was going on. At first, the manager wouldn't say much, until the guy pretended he knew the woman whose room they were clearing out. That's when it got funny. The manager asked him how to get in touch with Mary Maloney, and the dumb shit got in a huff trying to cover his tracks. It escalated. The manager called the cops, and the surveillance team hauled ass — all four of them in one car. They're definitely working for the Savannah target; we trailed them to his office.

"Our team got good pictures of the four people. We figured that might come in handy when you go after the Savannah target."

"Sounds like amateur hour," Mary said.

"Yeah. I thought you should know what kind of talent you could expect to run up against when the time comes."

"Did you send my text to the Russian?"

"We did. We sent it while all the excitement about the motel room was going on — around noon. There's still no reply from the Russian, but the burner phone he's using has moved since the last exchange. *Anastasia* is underway; she's running north along the coast, close enough to shore that the burner phone was still on the network. But then the phone disappeared. They probably ditched it."

"You sure about that, Aaron?" I asked. "They're not faking that?"

"Great minds, Finn. We had the same thought, but we spotted *Anastasia* in the same position as the phone. She's blasting along at 20 knots, a mile or two off the beach. Maybe they're headed for Savannah, figuring to catch up with you there. We're keeping an eye on their Savannah operation to see what they're up to."

"Keep an eye on the boat, too," I said. "At 20 knots, it wouldn't take them long to get to Charleston."

"Right," Aaron said. "But we're doing everything we can to make them think Savannah's the target."

"Okay. Anything else related to the motel?" I asked.

"No. Ready to talk about the mission?"

"Yes. Tell us about our Charleston target," I said.

"Jeremy Theroux runs a shipping company," Aaron said. "It's a family business; he inherited it. He's the fourth generation Theroux to run the operation. He's turned it into a real power-house in the industry.

"Until his father died and Jeremy took over, it was Theroux Shipping, Inc. Jeremy rebranded the company. The new name is SeaConnect Intermodal Corporation. They're into everything related to moving stuff around the globe.

"They do it all when it comes to logistics, including moving contraband. Illegal drugs, cash, people, stolen goods, prohibited exports, arms — If it can be bought and sold, Jeremy can move it from where it is to where his customers want it. They handle pickup and delivery, warehousing, consolidation, customs brokerage, and they move goods on land, sea, and in the air."

"Okay," I said. "And I gather Jeremy lives and works here in Charleston. Is that right?"

"He lives there, yes. He travels a lot, though, mostly by private jet. He lives in the old family home, an antebellum mansion on Battery Street overlooking the harbor. It's on the National Register of Historic Places. You won't have any trouble finding it.

He has live-in security and uses an armored limo to commute to his office a few blocks away. Not an easy target."

"What about the office?" I asked.

"It's in an old three-story warehouse that's been renovated and turned into an office/condo complex. He owns it, and the top floor is his headquarters. The rest is rented out."

"Married?" Mary asked.

"Yes, technically."

"Technically?"

"His wife doesn't spend a lot of time there. They have another house in Washington, D.C., where she stays."

"Good," I said. "Less chance of collateral damage, then."

"Children?" Mary asked.

"Two, in college. A girl at the University of Virginia, and a boy at William and Mary."

"What else?" I asked.

"He's in a long-term relationship with his secretary. She practically lives at the house on Battery Street. And that's probably enough to get you started. There's a package on its way to you via courier; you should get it in a couple of hours. All the details we have are in there, along with photographs. It's on paper with copies on a memory stick. You going to be in your room this evening?"

"We're about to go out for dinner," I said. "Otherwise, yes."

"I'll have the courier call to make sure you're home before she delivers it. Once you've taken a look, call me with any questions."

"Wait," Mary said. "You said he travels a lot. What's his schedule like over the next few days?"

"He just got back from a swing through Southeast Asia. The plane's laid up for a routine inspection until next week. He's probably recovering from jet lag while that happens. Then all bets are off, so you probably want to move fast. Unless you're thinking about knocking the plane out of the sky."

"Not my first choice," I said.

"Nor mine," Mary said.

"All right, then. Have a nice dinner, and call if I can help."

"Thanks. We'll be in touch," I said, disconnecting the call.

"Ready for dinner, sailor?"

"Yes, siren."

18

"THEY'RE JUST LEAVING THE HOUSE," I SAID, WATCHING THE Mercedes pull out onto Battery Street.

Mary and I split up after an early breakfast. I was watching Theroux's house; Mary was across the street from his office. We were in the early stages of our reconnaissance, in constant touch using throwaway cellphones with Bluetooth earpieces.

"Okay, I'm all set," she said. "Figure it'll take them 15 minutes to get here. Traffic's a nightmare."

"I'll head up your way," I said. "I doubt there's any point in my staying here, now that he's left for the office."

"What about his secretary? She with him?" Mary asked. "And what kind of car?"

"Yes. I saw them both get in the limo. It's a dictator's classic — big old black stretch Mercedes — you can't miss it. Probably couldn't stop it with an antitank weapon."

"Okay. You walking or taking a cab? Traffic stinks, seriously. I just got here. Probably would have been quicker to walk, in hindsight."

"That's what I'll do, then. Might as well keep the connection up, huh?"

"Sure," Mary said. "Nobody pays any attention to people talking to themselves any more. Every other person on the sidewalk has some kind of ear...unh..."

"Mary?"

I heard one more soft groan followed by a few seconds of silence. Then another woman's voice said, "I think she's fainted or something." I turned up the volume and started to jog up the sidewalk along Battery Street. Theroux's office was less than a mile away; the automobile traffic was bumper to bumper, and it was moving at a crawl.

I heard a man's voice in my ear now. "Step back, please. Give us a little room. I'm a doctor. The ambulance is on its way."

"Oh, good," the woman's voice said. "She was just standing here at the bus stop, and the next thing I knew, she collapsed."

"Okay," the man's voice said. "She'll be all right — pulse and respiration are strong. We'll — "

The sound of a siren cut him off. Ten seconds later, he said, "Okay, good. You got here quick. I'm Doctor Little. Vitals are strong. Let's get her to the ER and see what's going on. I'll ride with you."

"Okay, Doc. Just let us get her on the gurney, here."

There was another groan, louder than the conversation. That was Mary. Then the ambulance attendant again. "Okay, everybody give us a little room, please."

I could hear people in the background, speculating about what happened as the EMTs rolled her into the ambulance and closed the door.

"Let's haul ass," the doctor said. "With all those damn people, somebody may have called 911."

I heard a blast on the siren.

"Kill the siren," the doctor said. "No need to attract more attention."

I heard a response, probably from the driver, but I couldn't make out the words. Then the doctor spoke again.

"Yeah, okay. Well, we're clear of the crowd now, so cool it. It's okay if it takes a while to get to the boat; it'll give her time to come around. Better if she can stagger aboard under her own power. Anybody sees us, they'll just figure she's still drunk from last night. They would be more likely to remember somebody bein' carried aboard on a stretcher."

There was more conversation I couldn't understand, and then the doctor's voice said, "Gimme those blackout sunglasses. Might as well get them on her before she comes around. She don't need to see any of us, let alone the boss man."

There was a rustling sound, and then, "Shit," the doctor said. "Bitch was on the phone. One of them Bluetooth ear — "

A click told me he broke the connection. I stopped running and pulled my encrypted phone from the pocket of my shorts. Placing a call to Aaron, I crossed my fingers that he would pick up.

"Finn?"

"Yeah. We got a problem. Somebody snatched Mary while she was watching Theroux's office. She's in an ambulance with three guys, and they're taking her to 'the boat.' I need you to track this cellphone number I'm about to give you; find out where 'the boat' is."

I gave him the number of the throwaway that Mary was using to communicate with me. His keyboard clicked as he entered the digits, and then he spoke.

"Okay. That's in the works, but I can probably short-circuit this. *Anastasia* is in the City Marina, right downtown. Got in about dawn. Think that's the boat?"

"You got somebody watching her?"

"Yeah, but they're not tactical. They'll be no help beyond observation."

"That's okay. I'll hang up and haul ass to the marina. I'll call back when I get there, but if they get there first with Mary, you call me."

"Got it. Bye."

I broke into a run, pacing myself for a seven-minute mile. Given the traffic, I should easily beat the ambulance to the marina. As I ran, I considered what to do when I got there. If Mary's captors were trying to avoid notice, they would probably park the ambulance and walk to *Anastasia*. Then again, I didn't know much about the boat. A lot of big motor yachts carried golf carts, or even vans and cars. Was *Anastasia* that big? And did I remember that the City Marina offered courtesy golf carts?

I would have answers soon enough. My best chance to rescue Mary would probably be when they took her out of the ambulance. My guess was they shot her with a tranquilizer dart. From what I overheard, they expected her to regain consciousness by the time they got where they were going. But she might still be dopey; I couldn't count on her help.

There was the bogus doctor, and probably two men pretending to be ambulance attendants. They wouldn't be expecting trouble, especially by the time they got to the marina. The people on *Anastasia* would be waiting for them, though. They would most likely call somebody aboard the boat to let them know about their captive. That was another argument for hitting them as soon as they arrived at the marina.

Checking the street signs, I could see I was only two minutes from the marina. I wondered where the ambulance was. Aaron would probably know by now, but I didn't want to stop running long enough to call him. It didn't matter at this point. I would either beat them to the marina, or not. If not, they would have Mary.

I pondered that. The snatch removed any doubt; they wanted something from her. If they wanted to kill her, she would be dead by now. But they were planning on taking her aboard 'the boat' to meet the boss man. She was probably safe enough for the moment.

My instinct was to rescue her, but I reminded myself that one of our options was for her to accept the Russian's invitation to a meeting. Should I let that happen? I might not have a choice, but then again, I might. I wished that I could brainstorm this with her and Aaron and Mike, but that was a luxury I didn't have.

The downside to letting their plans go forward was clear enough. Mary was in danger; the only question was how much. What were the potential downsides of my rescuing her?

And then there was the question of how they knew where to find her to begin with. I put that aside; it would keep. The more critical question was whether I should take her away from her captors.

By now, I was jogging across the marina parking lot, heading for the entrance to the docks. That made a good choke point; the large yachts were tied on the outside of the face dock, and the only access was via a footbridge at the entrance. I found a park bench and leaned against it while I caught my breath. I kept an eye on the traffic out on Lockwood Drive, watching for the ambulance to turn into the parking lot.

After a couple of minutes, I got worried enough to call Aaron. "Yeah, Finn," he answered.

"I'm at the marina. No sign of the ambulance."

"They took a detour, but don't worry. The last couple of fixes on that phone still show it headed in your direction. My bet is they ditched the ambulance. It was stolen; they probably switched to a car."

"When did they steal the ambulance?"

"A couple of hours ago. Looks like they planned this well in advance."

"Yeah. I was just wondering how they found her. Hang on; a cab just pulled into the lot, headed this way. Gotta go. Call you later."

I watched as the cab cruised through the lot, expecting it to pull up near where I waited. Instead, it turned into an open parking place close to the marina entrance, and the driver got out. He was wearing an EMT uniform. He opened the left rear door and leaned into the back seat.

I walked toward the cab as fast as I could without attracting his attention. As I got within a few feet of the cab's back bumper, I could see the other man helping the driver get Mary out of the back seat. She wasn't unconscious, but she was too groggy to give them much help.

I made my decision. If I set up the scene properly, rescuing her wouldn't tell the Russian anything he didn't already know. They would think she escaped by herself. They knew that when she was O'Hanlon's prisoner in Martinique, she killed him and a half-dozen of his thugs all by herself. The Russian would just figure his boys got careless. How dangerous could one average-sized girl be, anyway?

I waited until they got her out of the back seat. The driver was struggling to support her. Her knees were wobbling and her head was lolling around. I rushed the driver from behind and caught his chin in one hand and the back of his head in the other. I snapped his neck before he knew I was there. I dropped him and reached for Mary. She gave me a vacant grin, gurgled something, and collapsed on top of the dead driver.

The second man was getting out of the back seat, trying to point his pistol at me when I kicked him in the face. He fell back into the cab, and I took his pistol. I dragged the dead man out from under Mary and shoved him into the back seat on top of the other one, closing the door.

The driver's door was still open, the engine running. I reached in and popped the trunk. I stepped over Mary and ran around the back of the cab, opening the right rear door. I dragged the man I kicked in the face out and helped him into the trunk, slamming the lid. I closed the right rear door and went back to Mary, loading her into the front seat and shoving her across to the passenger side.

Taking a quick look around to make sure nobody was watching, I got behind the wheel and drove out of the parking lot. I turned left on Lockwood Drive and headed out of town, following the signs toward Drayton Hall Plantation. If memory served, there was some undeveloped, swampy land not too far from there.

As I drove, Mary began to recover, collecting herself enough to sit up and look around.

"Wha' happen?" she asked, frowning. "Finn?"

"Yes. You're okay. Can you fasten your seat belt?"

She looked down and felt around for it, finally getting herself strapped in. "Where goin'?"

"I'm looking for a private spot. I want to ask your friend a question or two."

"My frien'?"

"Three men kidnapped you while you were watching Theroux's office."

"They did? When?"

"Oh, maybe an hour ago. They drugged you somehow."

"Oh. Who drugged me, again?"

"They probably work for the Russian. You remember the Russian?"

"Sniper? Right?"

"Uh-huh. Don't worry about it right now. Just rest. It'll all come back to you."

"You drivin' a taxi."

"Yep. They had you in an ambulance at first, but I guess they figured this wouldn't attract as much attention."

"Oh," she said.

Draping her left arm over the seat back, she strained against the seatbelt, peering out the back window and then down at the man with the broken neck.

"Somebody followin' us," she said.

I checked the mirrors. "I don't see anybody."

"He's in the back seat," she whispered.

"Oh, don't mind him. He's dead. There's a live one in the trunk."

"You stole the cab?"

"I'm just borrowing it. I think these guys probably stole it. You rest now, okay? I need to make a phone call."

"Okay," she said, leaning back and closing her eyes.

I took my encrypted phone from my pocket and called Aaron.

"What's happening, Finn?"

"I've got Mary, plus one dead body and one live prisoner."

"Where are you?"

"Heading for the sticks on the southwest outskirts of Charleston, looking for a dirt road."

"A dirt road?"

"I want to question the prisoner. Besides, I need to give Mary time to wake up from whatever they gave her."

"How the hell did they find her?"

"That's one of the questions I want to ask him. My working assumption is they staked out both targets — Savannah and Charleston. Given how many times Mary was in the hands of O'Hanlon's bunch, they probably have pictures of her."

"You said she was watching his office when they grabbed her?"

"Yes. I was watching his house. My bet is they had surveillance on both places, but they don't know about me. At least, not enough to recognize me."

"I guess they do now, though."

"Why do you say that?"

"You said there were three of them. You only accounted for two just now."

"Oh. Yeah. The third guy's probably ditching the ambulance. He never saw me. These two pulled up to the marina in a cab, with Mary. I killed one, saved the other to answer questions. The dead one's dressed like an ambulance attendant. The one pretending to be a doctor was giving orders. He's in the trunk, awaiting my pleasure."

"Okay. Do you need for me to do anything?"

"Yes. You said the surveillance people in Charleston weren't tactical, right?"

"Right. Why? You need muscle?"

"No. I need a ride. After I'm through with my friend in the trunk, I'll leave him and his buddy out in the sticks with the cab. Can one of your watchers pick up our rental car at the B&B and come get us?"

"Sure. Where and when?"

"I'll let you know. Probably be about an hour. I'll call you."

"What about ID? And the B&B? You skipping out?"

"No. Not unless I find out from this jerk that they know about our cover. There's no reason to think they do. Mary can disguise herself before we go back to the room, and we'll figure out the next step from there. Okay?"

"Yes. That makes sense."

"Good, Aaron. This looks like a nice, deserted spot right here. I might as well pull off into the bushes and get to work."

"Okay. I'll have somebody pick up your rental car now, and we'll be waiting for your call."

"Good enough. Thanks, Aaron."

19

"THAT SHOULD DO IT," I SAID, AS MARY MODELED HER NEW appearance for me.

"Like it?" she asked, fluffing her coal-black hair and blowing me an exaggerated kiss.

"Let's just say it's an effective disguise."

"That bad, huh?"

"You're a different woman, that's for sure."

She laughed. "That's the idea. Think I look enough different from the pictures in his phone?"

"Yes."

"Enough different so we can go back to the B&B? This place is filthy."

"Sure. Pack up your stuff."

"Do we need to check out?"

"No. I gave the clerk 50 bucks. She said we could stay as long as we wanted — 'even overnight,' she said, like that might be a big deal. We might as well get our money's worth. You sure you don't want to fool around?"

"Shut up, Finn. I may look like I belong in a place like this now, but I'm not staying here any longer. Not even with you, sailor. Let's go."

We were in a fleabag motel on US Highway 17, around 20 minutes southwest of Charleston. After Aaron's people brought our rental car to us out in the swamp, Mary was alert enough to deal with changing her appearance.

We found a suburban shopping area where she bought a few clothes and cosmetics. Then we checked into this place so that she could dye her hair. With the coal-black hair and a thick application of cheap makeup, she was a different woman.

"Yes, ma'am," I said.

Once we were in the car headed back into town, she asked, "Where's his phone? Did you keep it?"

"Yes. It's in that fanny pack I tossed in the back seat. Why?"

She loosened her seatbelt enough to reach over the seat back. Retrieving the pack, she unzipped it and took out the smartphone her captor was carrying.

"What's the code?"

I rattled off the six-digit security code he gave me before he died. She unlocked the phone.

"Looking for anything in particular?" I asked.

"No. Just curious to see what's here. And I wanted to see the pictures of me."

"You used to be pretty."

"That's not why I want to see them, wiseass."

"No?"

"No. I thought maybe I could tell where they were taken. Did he say how he got them?"

"Lavrov gave them to him."

Uri Lavrov was the Russian, at least that was the name he used with the man I interrogated.

"Wonder why he used the name Vasily Zaytsev with me that time?" Mary asked, as she scrolled through the pictures on the phone.

"Maybe we'll get to ask him before this is over. It was probably just on a whim, though," I said.

"Who was he, anyway? The guy you questioned. I remember you working on him, but I was too out of it to catch a lot of what he said."

"Johnny Davies was his name. Grew up in the sticks in western North Carolina, joined the Marines. Did two tours in Iraq. Got out of the Marines and signed up with an outfit that did contract dirty work in Iraq. Met a guy in a bar there who recruited him to go back to the States to work for Lavrov. Lavrov was already in the U.S., and he was putting together a team of people like Davies.

"There were six of them staying on *Anastasia*. Six American mercenaries, that is. Davies said the crew is Russian — eight men and four women. Plus Lavrov and his main squeeze. Davies was in charge of the mercenaries, according to him. Lavrov used them for basic muscle. He wanted Americans so they wouldn't attract attention."

"Did you ask him about the hits? Where they broke all the victims' bones?"

"Yes. Davies knew about it; he was there, both times. But one of the Russians did it. A former *Spetsnaz* officer. Davies said everybody was scared of him — even the other Russians. Said he was a psycho."

"You got a lot out of Davies," Mary said.

"Once guys like that realize they're toast, they get chatty. They know the longer they talk, the longer they get to keep breathing."

"I don't remember hearing him scream. How did you get him to talk?"

"He knew the score. The smart ones cave right away. They know they're about to die; why not take the easy way out? Guy like that knows what's going to happen. He's been on the other side. Once he was sure there was no escape, it was easier to answer the questions. There's no loyalty there, and no reward for suffering. That's not true with zealots, but Davies was no zealot. Just a thug."

"There's not much in the phone besides the pictures of me. Why did you keep it?"

"I thought we might want to use it to send the Russian a message."

Mary chuckled. "Anything in particular?"

"We've got time to think about that. Once we're back at the B&B, we can call Aaron and talk it over with him and Mike."

"Lavrov must be wondering what happened to Davies and the other man," Mary said.

"Oh, he's got a pretty good idea by now. There were two men with Davies."

"Two? What happened to the other one?"

"When they shot you with whatever it was, you were on the phone with me. Remember?"

"Not really. A lot's come back, but I don't remember that." She frowned and shook her head.

"Don't worry about it. It can take time. It doesn't matter, anyway."

"Tell me what happened, Finn."

"We split up. I was watching Theroux's house, and you staked out his office."

"I remember that, and calling you when I got there. But everything's fuzzy after that."

I filled her in on what I heard before Davies found her phone and disconnected our call.

"So I was in an ambulance?"

"Yes. A stolen one. Once they got you away from the area where they snatched you, they switched to the cab. Stolen, too, no doubt. The one driving the ambulance dropped you and the other two off at the cab and ditched the ambulance somewhere. I'm sure he's made his way back to *Anastasia* by now."

"But he wouldn't know what's happened, right? With you?"

"With me, probably not. Not unless somebody on *Anastasia* was watching for the cab to show up at the marina. And I don't think that's the case. If it were, they would have tried to follow us when I drove away in the cab."

"Then all they know is that Davies and the other man and the cab are missing, with me as their prisoner."

"They may know more than that," I said. "Davies was checking in with somebody on *Anastasia*. One of the women, he said, but her English was marginal, and he didn't speak enough Russian to help. So the third man ditched the ambulance and went back to the boat. That much is almost certain. Beyond that, Davies said he checked in with the woman when they got you in the ambulance, and again when they got you in the cab. At that point, he told her they would be back on *Anastasia* with you in about 15 minutes. He said she didn't seem to get all he was telling her, but she might have been recording it, to play back for Lavrov."

"Then they would know about when the cab got to the marina," Mary said. "They would have started looking then, right?"

"Maybe. We don't know; Davies didn't know. It depends on whether the woman understood, and how long it took for her to get through to Lavrov. See what I mean?"

"Then they would have wondered why Davies wasn't back and tried to call him, right?" She picked up his smartphone again.

"I already checked. No missed calls in there. Nothing after his last call, which was about 10 or 15 minutes before they got to the marina. Like I said, we don't know what they know, or when they found out things were off the rails. But they definitely know by now. And they may or may not know Davies made it to the marina. They also know that you were on the phone with somebody when they grabbed you. They won't know how much I overheard of their conversation in the ambulance."

"Thanks, Finn."

"You're welcome. Sorry I don't know more about it all."

"Oh. Not for filling me in. I appreciate that, but I meant

thanks for rescuing me. I feel like a real loser, letting myself get blindsided like that."

"Don't be hard on yourself. Sometimes stuff happens that's beyond your control."

"Yeah. We call that screwing up. If it weren't for you — "

"If it weren't for me, you would have gotten to meet the Russian by now. I'm not sure rescuing you was smart."

"What?!"

"Take it easy. One thing I thought of while I was running to the marina was that they wanted something from you. They weren't out to do you any harm — not at that point. They could have killed you with a lot less trouble than it took to capture you. We already know Lavrov wanted to meet with you. Oh sure, he was heavy-handed about it, but that's just his style, right?"

She was glaring at me. I felt like her stare was burning a dime-sized hole in the side of my head.

"Why did you decide to save me, then, Mr. Ice-Water-in-Your-Veins?"

"The opportunity presented itself, and I figured there wasn't really a downside. Besides, it would — "

"Well, that's great, you asshole. Not really a downside to saving me. I'm so glad. You're... I've got a good mind to..."

She clenched her jaws and crossed her arms, turning away from me and staring out the passenger side window.

Let her fume, Finn. She's shaken up and feeling vulnerable, and you really pissed her off. You didn't do such a hot job of explaining your thought process, but at this stage, it's better to let her cool down. You can try again in a little while. Meanwhile, get your shit together and figure out how to explain what you were trying to get across to her.

20

"Sorry I didn't do a better job of explaining my thought process earlier," I said. "I was more than a little stressed out."

Mary gave me a tired smile. We were back in our room at the B&B. She was sitting on the edge of our bed, and I was in a rocking chair, facing her.

"I'm sorry I overreacted, Finn. I understand what you meant, now that I've calmed down."

"I was trying to steel myself for what might happen if I didn't manage to get you away from them — to rationalize my failure, if it came to that. But there was never a moment when I wasn't committed to freeing you if I could."

"I know. I get that. I'm glad it worked out the way it did. You okay?"

"Me?" I asked. "Sure. I'm not the one that got doped up and kidnapped."

"That's not what I meant, and you know it. I meant are you okay with me."

"Yes. Thanks for understanding my clumsy words."

"I love you, sailor."

"And I love you, siren." I moved to the bed, sitting next to her, and put an arm around her shoulders.

"Finn?"

"Yes?"

"We should call Aaron before we... Well, you know."

"You're right. But before we do that, we should get our act together as far as what to do about Lavrov — and Theroux, for that matter."

"Yes," Mary said. "I have some ideas."

"Tell me."

"Okay, but first, do you think his people spotted you this morning? Outside Theroux's house, I mean?"

"I don't see how. I looked just like all the other tourists walking around and gawking at the sights. And Davies said they thought you always worked alone. He set it all up. He assigned one man to watch for you at the house, and one at the office. The one at the office spotted you arriving in a taxi and called Davies. Davies was waiting in the ambulance, about halfway between the two places. Once he got the call, he staged the ambulance close to the office and joined his man there. When Davies arrived, they took you down."

"And you don't think they saw you at the marina? When you hijacked the cab?"

"No. They would have made an effort to stop me; I was watching for that. I saw no sign of them. That was sloppy of them, but I guess they were overconfident. Why?"

"You'll see when I tell you my plan. Ready?"

"Ready. Let's hear it."

"Okay. Those pictures Davies had of me — they were from Martinique, shot aboard Frankie Dailey's motor yacht. I recognized stuff in the background. So Lavrov has to know what happened there. Otherwise, he wouldn't have the pictures, right?"

"Right. You think he got them after the fact, somehow?"

"That's the only way. He had to get them from somebody in

the local government down there. Those were shot less than a minute before I mowed down the O'Hanlon bunch. They were screwing around, trying to pose with me, like the sick, S&M crap you see on the web. That's how I got my hands on the pistol I used. But anyway, my idea is to play on my reputation."

"How?" I asked.

"I wasted O'Hanlon and six of his boys, single-handed. That should give me a little credibility when I text Lavrov. Especially when my text comes from Johnny Davies's phone, don't you think?"

"What are you going to say to him?"

"Try this for a start: *'You should hire better people, Lavrov. But don't feel too bad; there aren't many who can measure up to my standards. I took out O'Hanlon and six of his best, so your second string in Charleston wasn't much of a challenge. Johnny Davies sang like a scared little bird, in case you're wondering. I see why you want to meet with me, after what he told me. But you need me more than I need you. If you really want to win me over to your side, take out Theroux for me — save me the trouble. Then maybe we can talk — but only if you upgrade your talent. I don't work with amateurs — or for them. Prove you're not a loser. Kill Theroux, and that moron in Savannah, too. It's in your best interest anyway, because if I kill them, they'll tell me all about you first. I can guarantee that. If I get to them first, I'll assume you're not interested in a partnership. And that could be the kiss of death for you, Uri.'"*

"Wow," I said. "Gutsy."

"Yeah, well, why not? As the man I love says, 'What's the downside?'"

"Ouch. I thought we were past that."

"We are. Sorry, but I couldn't resist, once I got my adrenalin up."

"Uh-huh. I like it. You've been thinking about that for a while, haven't you?"

"Yes. I was thinking along those lines before Lavrov screwed up. Now he's played right into our hands."

"What happens if he buys it?"

She squinted for a few seconds. "I'm not sure what you're asking — buys it, how?"

"Let's say he kills Theroux and the moron in Savannah — better if we use the moron's name in the text. Then what?"

"I haven't worked that out yet. You think he'll kill them?"

"I don't know. He just might. He knows they're your targets, and now he knows you can connect them with him. If you made Davies talk, he'll worry that Theroux and the other one might spill something important if you get to them first."

"That would be so cool, wouldn't it? Get him to do our work for us?"

"Yes. But there's still the question of what happens afterward."

"We've got a couple of days to think about that. Should we get hold of Aaron?"

"Let's send him a text, give him a chance to line up Mike and Bob, maybe. I think they should be in on this."

"Okay. That makes sense."

"I'll ask him to set up a call around six, if he can," I said.

"It's only four o'clock. What are we going to do for two hours?"

"Work off some of that adrenalin you were complaining about, and then maybe take a nap."

"Hurry up and send your text, sailor."

"Yes, ma'am. I hear the siren's song."

———————

"Aaron?" I asked, as I answered the call on my special phone.

"Yes. Mike's here, too. Bob's tied up; he sends his best."

"Good evening, gentlemen," Mary said.

"Hello, Mary," Mike said. "We heard a little about your adventure. You doing okay?"

"Yes. I'm back to normal now, thanks."

"Good. Aaron said you want to discuss where we go from here. Aaron, anything before we get started?"

"Not really. *Anastasia* is still in Charleston. They're in the middle of a big fuel delivery — got hoses run from a tanker truck ashore. Maybe they're prepping to leave, or maybe it's just a convenient place to refuel."

"Lavrov must have figured out that his boys weren't coming home by now," I said.

"Lavrov?" Mike asked.

"The Russian," I said. "That's one of the things we wanted to talk about. I got a little information from the guy who kidnapped Mary."

"Tell us," Mike said.

I gave them the details of what we learned since our last conference call.

"Now we've got a name for him," Aaron said. "I can try to dig up background on him. What's his first name?"

"Uri," I said.

"How are you two feeling about Theroux?" Mike asked. "Think we need to let things settle down before you take him out?"

"You should hear Mary's idea before we get into that," I said. "She's thinking we should twist Lavrov's tail. Mary?"

Mary explained her idea for provoking Lavrov. "So he not only *heard* about me from O'Hanlon, but he's got a good idea that I wiped out O'Hanlon and his team in Martinique," she said, in conclusion.

"If he takes the bait," Mike said, "how would you make a deal with him?"

"I'm not sure. It depends on what we want. Are we setting him up for a hit, or are we trying to learn more about what he's doing?"

"Right," Mike said. "I'll have to kick that around with the

others here, but I suspect we'll want to infiltrate his operation before we eliminate him. He may have more going on than just picking up the pieces of O'Hanlon's business. Do you see yourself working undercover? I mean, as part of his operation?"

"Maybe," Mary said. "If I convince Lavrov to take out Theroux and the man in Savannah, that sends a strong signal about how committed he is to making me part of his team."

I started to speak, but Mary nudged me and shook her head. I coughed instead.

"You're proposing to admit to him you've been killing his people," Aaron said.

"He knows that already; I was staking out Theroux when his troops snatched me this morning, remember? But I can't see how he would know about Phorcys. Can you?"

"Maybe not now," Mike said. "But if you were joining his team, it would be reasonable for him to ask who you were working for. How would you answer that?"

"I'm open to suggestions," Mary said. "I thought about telling him I was part of the same organization as Finn, but that's risky. If I could get away with it, there's some upside, though."

"It's beyond risky, Mary. He penetrated that whole chain of command," Mike said, with exaggerated patience.

"Yes, but we don't know how much he knows about the working level. He probably didn't get that far down the food chain."

"That's a wild assumption," Mike said. "And what's the upside you mentioned?"

"Maybe I could bring Finn along to watch my back."

"No. That's not a good idea," Mike said. "That increases the chance he'll see through your cover. If you go undercover, it will have to be solo. I'm not sure you're ready. How do you feel about that?"

"It's the only way I've ever worked," Mary said, the color rising in her cheeks. "The Finn thing was just an idea."

"A bad idea," Mike said. "Forget it. If you go, you go alone. But we're not even close to doing that. Let's consider what Lavrov might do if we send that text you outlined for us. Finn, you've been quiet. How do you think Lavrov would react to that?"

"He knows Mary was poised to hit Theroux, and he knows her track record. He'll have to figure that Theroux is dead meat. Ditto for the man in Savannah. Mary makes a good case that one of those two could be made to talk. That makes them liabilities to Lavrov once we send the text, so he might take Mary's suggestion and kill them. What do we know about them, anyway?"

"What are you looking for, Finn?" Aaron asked. "Something specific? Leverage over them?"

"No. I was wondering if we could set one of them up — make Lavrov think one of them was trying to sell him out. Something independent of the text."

"Now that's an interesting thought," Mike said. "You mean to encourage Lavrov to kill them to win Mary over?"

"Something like that, yes. Or in case Lavrov doesn't bite, to decide whether we should interrogate them. Does the man in Savannah have a name, by the way?"

"James Stringfellow," Mike said. "Aaron, see what you can turn up that we might use to frame them — either one. Okay, Finn. What else might Lavrov do if we send him that text?"

"There's always the chance he'll decide to kill Mary, given what we did to his boy, Davies. But I think he wants something from her. I'm not so sure I buy Mary's theory that he wants her as an enforcer."

Mary kicked my ankle, her eyes flashing. Her face was red. I put a finger over her lips and said, "As good as she is, he has at least one *Spetsnaz* killer with him. We've seen evidence of how effective that guy is — twice, recently. So my gut tells me there's more behind his wanting to meet Mary. Could he be looking for a copy of O'Hanlon's files? Or the money she stole?"

"Now that's a thought," Mike said. "It could be either one, but since Lavrov was working with O'Hanlon before O'Hanlon died, wouldn't he already have the information from the files?"

"Not necessarily," I said. "O'Hanlon wanted those files himself, remember?"

"But only to make sure they didn't fall into the wrong hands," Aaron said. "Right, Mary? O'Hanlon hired you to retrieve them from Dailey, didn't he?"

Mary took a deep breath and let it out before she answered.

"Mary?" Mike asked. "You still with us?"

"Yes, but Finn's right. Remember, the Daileys ran that whole part of O'Hanlon's operation. Francis X. Dailey was the bagman. O'Hanlon sent me in there to get the records because he thought the Daileys were skimming. He wanted them dead, but he wanted the files, first. Dailey had the only copy."

"Lavrov's trying to take over what O'Hanlon left behind," I said. "But for all he knows, Mary's working for somebody else with the same idea. Lavrov knows O'Hanlon was trying to get the files from Mary, so he figures she still has them, or has access to them."

"We've covered a lot of ground," Mike said. "I think we need to digest this. Let's give Aaron time to look into Lavrov, now that we have a name for him. I like the idea of sending him a provocative text, but that will keep for a little while. We're not ready to take him out yet, but it wouldn't be a bad thing to shake him up. If we get him rattled, he's likely to make mistakes. Let's talk again in the morning. Is nine o'clock okay?"

"Good for me," Aaron said. "I can at least get a start on Lavrov between now and then."

Mary caught my eye and nodded, but her jaws were clenched.

"Good for us, too," I said. "Good evening."

After I broke the connection, Mary and I went out to dinner.

21

"I DIDN'T WANT TO SAY ANYTHING OVER DINNER," I SAID, "BUT NOW that we're in private again, we need to talk."

Mary sat on the edge of the bed, looking up at me. "About?"

"This undercover business."

"You have some fresh ideas?"

I shook my head, struggling with what I wanted to say. "Not really, but the more I think about it, the less I like it."

"Why's that?"

"It's too dangerous, Mary."

She forced a laugh. "Come on, Finn. Of course it's dangerous. So what?"

"I don't want you to do it."

She frowned. "Wait a second. *You* don't want me to do it?"

I swallowed hard. *This isn't starting out well, Finn. Be careful.* "I love you, Mary. I don't want you taking that kind of risk. You'd be completely on your own, and — "

"Let's cut our losses. This was a bad idea," she snapped.

"I agree. Lavrov could — "

"I wasn't talking about that," she said.

"What were you talking about, then? What's a bad idea?"

"Us. It's not going to work, Finn."

"Us?"

"You and me. Us. I can't deal with this; I'm not yours to order around."

"I wasn't trying to — "

"Bullshit, Finn. You think I can't see you're trying to manipulate me? You have no right to say how I do my work. Or what risks I choose to take, either."

"Mary, let me explain, okay?"

She glared at me for several long seconds, her eyes flashing under her furrowed brow. At last, she nodded, but her expression didn't change.

"I've been doing this for almost as long as you've been alive." I paused. *Not a good start, Finn.* "Working undercover's a whole different game from killing people. It's a long-term thing; not something you do and put behind you. You have to turn yourself into a different person, and you can't look back at who you used to be. You really have to become whoever you're trying to be. It's a tough, dangerous game. You understand what I'm trying to say?"

"Better than you know. You don't have a clue about me, Finn. I've lived most of my life pretending to be somebody else. How much undercover work have *you* ever done? Be honest, now."

"Not much, but I've been — "

"Stop right there. I'm sorry, Finn. I never meant for you to fall in love with me — not like this. You were part of a job for me, remember? And you weren't supposed to get hurt. I was supposed to keep you safe so you could..." She shook her head. Her eyes filled with tears. "Oh, shit."

I sat down on the bed next to her and put my arm around her. She shrugged it off and stood up, moving to the little table in the corner. Pulling out a chair, she sat. I watched her, but she avoided looking me in the eye. Almost a minute passed before she spoke again.

"We're both professionals, Finn. We can do this; we have to

put our feelings aside. Our obligation is to Phorcys, now." She looked me in the eye, waiting.

I held her gaze, saying nothing.

"I'm sorry, Finn; I can't be responsible for how you feel about me, okay? I know you mean well, but this has to stop."

"What has to stop?"

"This emotional crap. It's going to get one of us killed. You know what I'm trying to say?"

"I'm not sure I do. What do you want from me?"

She shook her head. "Nothing. You have things you have to do. So do I. You haven't told me much about your history, but I've always worked alone. That's what makes me what I am. I can't have you tagging along, nipping at my heels and watching my back. It's too big a distraction. Don't you get that?"

I cleared my throat. "Working as part of a team is — "

"No, Finn. I don't need you to keep me safe, and I'm not a team player. I don't want to be worrying about what somebody else is doing. I'm not made that way."

"Okay. If that's the way you want to — "

"What I want doesn't enter into it," she said. "Neither does what you want. A loner — it's what I am. It's the way I work."

"Okay," I said, extending both hands, palms facing her, making a pushing motion. "Enough. Sorry I even brought it up. Forget I said anything. We've got a job to do."

"You did bring it up, though. It's out in the open; you can't put the toothpaste back in the tube, as they say."

"I don't think that cliché fits this situation. I — "

"And *we* don't have a job to do. *I* have a job to do. Maybe you have one, too. Maybe they're even related. But *I'm* the one who's in a position to infiltrate Lavrov's crowd, and there's no way I'm taking you along. Mike was right about that, even if he is a patronizing old bastard. I was dumb to even think about it; it's just as well he shot it down."

"Speaking of Mike," I said, "we don't know that they will want you to go undercover. Maybe we should see what's — "

"Uh-uh, Finn. This isn't just about whether I go undercover to penetrate Lavrov's operation, and you know it. It's about my independence. You don't call the shots for me; I thought you knew that. Neither does Phorcys — not unless *I* let them."

"I read you loud and clear, Mary. You do what you need to do. Don't worry about me."

"What? Now you're going to end our relationship because I won't let you boss me around?"

"I thought that's what you meant when you said it wasn't going to work, this thing between you and me."

"This *thing*?!" Her face turned red under her tan. "That's all our relationship is to you? *A thing*?!"

I took a deep breath and let it out slowly, counting to ten. This was one of those times when anything I said would be used against me. I might not know a lot about women, but I knew that much, for sure.

"Well?" she said, still flushed. "Don't you have anything to say for yourself?"

"This isn't the conversation I expected us to have, Mary. I'm sorry I've said the wrong things. I never meant to upset you. I — "

"I, I, I. It's all about you, isn't it? Well, I'm my own person, Finn. Not an extension of you. Got it?"

"Yes. I understand."

"Good. I need some space right now. I can't sit here with you; I'm too angry."

I nodded. "Do you want me to leave? Get a room of my own?"

"No." She stood up and began throwing her stuff in her duffle bag. "I'm outta here."

"What about the conference call in the morning?"

"I have my own secure phone, remember? I'll call Aaron and he can add me on. It's about time those bastards learned I'm not just a playmate for good old Finn." She stormed out and slammed the door behind her.

Well, boy, I guess you screwed the pooch on this one. You and your big mouth. She's right about one thing, though. We've got a job to do, and she's the one who's exposed.

At least as far as Lavrov knows, she's working alone, thanks to Johnny Davies's sloppy work. Since the people on Anastasia didn't have a lookout posted to see me hijack that cab, they don't know about my part in their failed kidnap attempt.

As Mary said, her killing Davies and then escaping would be consistent with why Lavrov said he wanted to hire her. He would assume that's what happened. It's a lot like what she did to O'Hanlon and his crew in Martinique, and Lavrov knows about that.

But I wasn't convinced that Lavrov's only interest was in Mary's skill as an assassin. The more we talked about it this afternoon, the more convinced I became that Lavrov was after those files she took from the Daileys. Given that, her likelihood of surviving an undercover assignment in his operation was slim, even as deadly as she was. No matter what he told her, he wasn't interested in her skill as an enforcer. By his reckoning, anyway, he wouldn't need another killer; he was well fixed with his *Spetsnaz* thugs. He would do whatever it took to make her hand over the files.

I could call Aaron and Mike now and share that worry with them, but I would feel obligated to let them know that Mary and I were on the outs. I wasn't comfortable doing that yet; I harbored a faint hope she and I could patch things up after a cool-down period.

All indications were that the folks at Phorcys were comfortable with the relationship Mary and I shared, but that could change in a hurry. If a lover's quarrel jeopardized our mission, I wasn't sure how Mike and Bob would deal with it, but I knew it wouldn't end well for Mary or for me. I would keep our personal problems out of their sight, and I was sure Mary would do the same. Despite her hot temper, she was a consummate professional.

The best I could do for her and Phorcys at this stage was to try to influence our plans to avoid her having a one-on-one meeting with Lavrov.

Before she entered into her current arrangement with Phorcys, she booked her contract kills through an agent who provided a buffer between her and her clients. From what she told me, she never met the people who hired her. Not only that, but she didn't even know their identity, nor did they know hers. It was via the broker that she began her work with Phorcys. If I were careful, I might be able to steer Phorcys and Mary to keep the broker between her and Lavrov.

Deciding to sleep on that, I turned down the bed and switched off the light.

22

"GOOD MORNING, AARON," I SAID, ANSWERING HIS CALL. I WAS BACK in the room at the B&B, having just returned from breakfast.

"Hi, Finn. Mary on the line?"

"Uh, no. She left after dinner last night on personal business. She said she'd get in touch with you this morning so you could add her on the call."

"You haven't seen her since dinner?" Mike asked.

"Good morning, Mike," I said. "That's right."

"Do you know where she went?"

"No; she goes her own way sometimes. Given what we do, I don't poke my nose into her business uninvited."

"I see. But she was going to call Aaron this morning, you say?"

"That's right. She mentioned it, specifically. Reminded me that she had her own secure phone."

"Right," Mike said. "Aaron?"

"Yes, sir?"

"See if you can reach her. Finn and I will hold."

"Yes, sir. I'll be right back."

"Finn?" Mike asked.

"Yes?"

"While we're waiting, do you have any more thoughts on what we were discussing yesterday?"

"You mean Mary's idea about sending the text to Lavrov?"

"Yes. Did you and Mary kick that around after we talked?"

"A little, yes. I'm not sure it's a good idea for her to join up with Lavrov. My take is that he wants the files she took from Dailey. This notion of her becoming his enforcer is a smoke-screen, in my opinion. He just wants to get his hands on her so he can force her to hand over the files."

"Uh-huh. What does she think about that?"

"She sees it differently. She makes the point that he knows she took out O'Hanlon and his team in Martinique. And as far as Lavrov knows, she killed Davies after she questioned him. We don't think Lavrov's people know I helped her escape. She's sure he wants her to sign on as his personal executioner."

"And you don't know where she is? What she's up to?"

"No, sir. But I'm surprised she — "

"Excuse me," Aaron said, rejoining our call.

"Did you reach her?" Mike asked.

"No. Her phone's been off the network since about nine last night."

"That's about when she left," I said.

"Can you track it?" Mike asked.

"No, sir."

"I thought these phones had independent GPS transponders," Mike said.

"They do," Aaron said, "But if the main battery is dead for more than a few hours, the auxiliary battery for the tracker will die. Or if the phone is shielded, the transponder can't get a GPS signal or a satellite query."

"Shielded? What's that mean?"

"Enclosed in a conductive container, for example. Say it's in the trunk of an automobile. That's not perfect, but it might be a good enough shield. Or if you want to be certain, you can stick it in a microwave oven. They're well-shielded by design, to keep radio frequency radiation inside."

"So it could be accidental or deliberate that we can't find her?"

"That's correct," Aaron said.

"All right," Mike said. "Let's put that aside for now, unless one of you has reason to think she might be in trouble."

"Okay," Aaron said. "I sent her a text, and I left her a voicemail, so when the phone comes back on the network, she'll know we're looking for her."

"Good enough," Mike said. "Finn's of the opinion that Lavrov's interested in Mary because he wants O'Hanlon's files, rather than wanting to use her as an enforcer. We were talking about that while you were trying to track her down. What's your take on that?"

"Well, it squares with what we've turned up on Lavrov so far. If he's who we think he is, he started out as *Spetsnaz* and went from there to the old KGB as an assassin. We don't know his real name; Lavrov's no doubt an alias. If we've got the right guy, he's been through a lot of identities. After the KGB became the FSB, he went into business for himself — at least in theory. As talented as Mary is, I doubt Lavrov's impressed with her. He's been surrounded with that kind of talent for most of his career, I expect."

"Okay. I talked this over with Bob Lawson last night. Without knowing what you just told us, he and I reached the same conclusion. The danger involved in sending Mary to infiltrate Lavrov's organization far outweighs the benefit. And I don't just mean danger to her. There's all sorts of exposure that could result.

"Having said that, we should string Lavrov along for as long as we can. Every interaction we have with him reveals more about what he's up to. Bob and I like the idea of using the phone you took from his boy Davies to send him a message, Finn. The question is what we say to him. We want to provoke him. Get him to stumble so we can learn more about him. Any ideas?"

"Yes," I said. "I've been wrestling with that. I agree that the risk to reward ratio argues against sending Mary into the lion's den, but I think her approach to setting the hook with Lavrov is sound."

"All right. Can you elaborate on that?" Mike asked.

"Sure. We should keep Mary's behavior in character. From what she's told me, she worked through a broker until she connected with us. She said that's how she did her first jobs with Phorcys, even."

"That's correct. But that was before you and Aaron came along. How much do you know about the broker? Either of you?"

"Nothing," Aaron said. "This is all new to me."

"Good," Mike said. "Your perspective will be untainted, then. Finn? How about you?"

"Not much more than I've told you. I picked up bits and pieces from her; she's not much for full disclosure."

Mike chuckled. "Nor should she be. What bits and pieces?"

"Well, let's see. The broker's a woman. She runs a double-blind operation, so Mary never knew the identity of her clients, and vice versa."

"Uh-huh," Mike said. "That tracks with our experience. Anything else?"

"Not really, but Mary made it sound convoluted. I can't remember all the twists and turns in the story, and I still have my doubts about some of what she said. The impression I got was that there were lots of cut-outs along the communications path. It almost sounded unworkable. Except I guess it worked. You'd know better than I, right?"

"Convoluted is a good way to describe it," Mike said. "And it did work. So what's your idea?"

"Well, Mary should be consistent in how she deals with Lavrov. If he wants to hire her, she should force him to go through the broker. She shouldn't deviate from her normal method of doing business. That's assuming that Lavrov doesn't know about her arrangement with us. Obviously, that's a deviation for her."

"Right," Mike said. "So we send him a text from Davies's phone, which he knows or suspects is in Mary's possession, and we set him on the path to the broker. Is that your idea?"

"Yes," I said. "Before we send the text, Aaron should be monitoring Lavrov's communications. If we know the number Davies used to send texts to Lavrov, you can monitor that, right, Aaron?"

"That's right. And once we've got a physical location for Lavrov, or for the receiving device, we can lock onto everything that goes in or out of the location. If he's using sophisticated encryption, we may not get much in the way of content, but connecting timing with location may be enough for us to figure out what's going on. Mike?"

"Yes?"

"How much do you and Bob know about this broker?"

"Enough. We can make this work. She's got a track record with us — the broker, that is. I don't want to say more."

"Can you get me the number of the cellphone Davies was using, Finn?" Aaron asked.

"Sure. Want me to just send you a text from it?"

"No, don't do that. It's possible that Lavrov's people are monitoring it somehow. We don't want to give them more reaction time than we need to. His phone's not powered up, is it?"

"I don't think so. Mary turned it off not long after we took it from him; we left it on long enough to see what was in it — the pictures of Mary from the O'Hanlon hit in Martinique, mostly. No recent call records. I'm not sure about texts. I was driving and she was still groggy, but I think she said there were text messages in there, probably from Lavrov, giving Davies his instructions. It was a cheap throwaway phone."

"That's fine," Aaron said. "Get me the number. You got a microwave in your room?"

"Yes."

"Stick it in there while you turn it on, and close the door against your arm. Look through the crack to get the number while it's powering up. As soon as you get the number, shut it off, okay? We don't want them to see it go on the network. Once I've got the number, we can spoof it and send Lavrov a message that appears to originate from that phone. We can make the phone's location anywhere we want."

"What about getting Lavrov's number from the phone? Don't I need to get that for you?"

"No. That will be in the call records from Davies's phone. We'll get that once we hack into the service provider's database. All I need is the number from Davies's phone."

"Okay, then. Hang on while I get it."

I looked through all our belongings that were in the room while Aaron and Mike waited. The phone was nowhere to be found.

"We've got a problem," I said. "I thought the phone was in the fanny pack I was wearing yesterday, but it's not there. I can't find it here in the room. Mary had it when we were in the car. I have a feeling it ended up in her stuff when she left last night."

"Uh-oh," Aaron said. "How about in your car?"

"I'll check and call you back, but I doubt that. Neither of us leaves stuff in the car. She was still dopey, though."

"Wait," Mike said. "Let's break off here. Bob should be out of his meeting by now. I'll go fill him in and talk with him about what we want to say to Lavrov while you two sort out this phone business."

"All right," I said.

"You call Aaron when you have the phone, Finn. Aaron?"

"Yes, sir?"

"You know how to reach me when you're ready."

"Yes."

"All right," Mike said. "We'll talk later."

I disconnected the call and put my secure phone in my pocket as I left the room. The car was in a small parking lot which was once part of the garden of the old house that was now the B&B. Five minutes later, I was back in the room. The phone wasn't in the car. There was only one place it could be, and that was in Mary's duffle bag, with Mary. Back in the room, I called Aaron.

"Finn?"

"Yeah. No luck on the phone. It must have ended up in Mary's stuff."

"Crap," Aaron said. "That's too bad, but it may not matter right now, anyway."

"Why's that?"

"I just heard from the surveillance team at the marina. The cops are all over *Anastasia*. My watcher is still trying to figure out what's going on. They've blocked off access to most of the face dock where she's tied up. Hang on; I'll patch you in to our call."

A few seconds passed, and then Aaron said, "Finn?"

"Yeah, I'm here."

"Josie?"

"Here."

"What's happening?" Aaron asked.

"The cops are stringing up yellow tape all over the place. Two ambulances just pulled up, and a crime scene van. Greg went in the marina office right before I called you to see what he could find out."

"Greg is part of Josie's surveillance team, Finn," Aaron said.

"Thanks," I said.

"Here," Josie said. "Greg's back. I'm giving him the phone."

There was a short, muffled conversation, and then a man's voice said, "Aaron?"

"Yeah, Greg. What's happening?"

"*Anastasia* was supposed to leave before dawn, but she didn't. The captain settled their bill last night before the office closed. The marina's expecting another big motor yacht this morning, and they need the dock space. The manager tried calling *Anastasia* on the radio and tried the captain's cellphone, too. He didn't get an answer, so he went aboard about 30 minutes ago. There are dead bodies; nobody alive on the boat — the manager freaked out, called the cops. That's solid intel, but I also picked up some rumors. Want to hear those?"

"Sure," Aaron said.

"Okay. A dozen bodies, everybody except the owner and his bodyguard. That came second-or-third-hand from the manager, by way of some of the staff. May or may not be accurate. Late yesterday, the captain asked the concierge here to book them dock space in Savannah for this afternoon, downtown, on the riverfront. That's solid. And that's about it."

"No word on the owner and his bodyguard?" I asked.

"Only that they haven't turned in the car they rented late yesterday."

"Can you find out any more about that car?" Aaron asked.

"Maybe. I'll check on it. Anything else?"

"Not right now. Both of you stay there and keep an eye on what happens. I want to know everything — facts, rumors, wild-ass guesses — everything."

"You got it, boss," Josie said. "Greg, let me know ASAP on that car. Get a copy of the rental agreement if you can."

"Right, Josie. I'm on it. Bye, y'all."

"Bye, Greg," Josie said. "Aaron, I'm going to ease in as close as I can get to the cops' access check point. I'll call as soon as we get anything new."

"Thanks, Josie."

There was a click on the line as she disconnected.

"Finn, you still there?"

"I'm here."

"What do you think?"

"No idea, Aaron. You gonna tell Mike and Bob?"

"Yes, right now. You want to stay on the line?"

"Not much. I'm going to see if I can find that missing cell-phone. And maybe figure out where Mary went. I'll have this phone with me. Keep me posted, okay?"

"You bet. Good luck with your search."

"Thanks. Talk with you later."

23

DESPITE WHAT I TOLD AARON A FEW MINUTES AGO, I WAS AT A LOSS as to how to find Mary. When we picked up our new identities in Orlando a few days ago, she became Mary Catherine Ryan, but that didn't mean much. Besides the identities provided by Phorcys, she had a collection of her own, stashed in lockboxes in various east-coast cities. Charleston was likely to be one of them, so she might well have a different name this morning. And then there was her skill at altering her appearance. She fooled me twice in the last two weeks.

She left here after dinner last night. That was too late for shopping in most places, but Charleston was a tourist town. Lots of souvenir shops stayed open late, and some stalls in the city market did, as well. I was thinking in terms of T-shirts, sweatshirts, hats — that kind of thing. She wouldn't have had a problem picking up accessories that would alter her appearance, even after nine p.m.

Since I didn't know what she looked like or what she was calling herself, all I could do was prowl places where she might hang out. Although I didn't mention it to Aaron, the slaughter on *Anastasia* screamed her name. From what Aaron's surveillance team reported, it bore a strong resemblance to the massacre she carried out on Frankie Dailey's motor yacht in Martinique.

Mary stuck around the scene in Martinique, watching for me to show up. Of course, back then she wasn't angry with me. But she was mercurial. She had probably cooled down by now, given what I suspected she did last night. Killing is a marvelous outlet for pent-up anger. I would stroll over to the marina and look at *Anastasia*. Maybe the scene would give me some insight, or maybe Mary would see me and get in touch.

It was still early for a tourist town; there weren't many people on the sidewalks. One girl sat on a bench at the bus stop half a block up the street from the B&B. Other than her, all the people I saw were couples, except for a few families with children.

As I got closer, I saw that the girl looked disheveled, her brown hair pulled back in a lank, greasy-looking ponytail. She wore dirty jeans, tattered running shoes, and a College of Charleston hooded sweatshirt that was too big for her. She kept her nose stuck in a book and didn't look up as I walked by.

I barely heard her as she mumbled, "Hey, mister. Help me out with some spare change?" I broke my stride and glanced down at her, but she didn't return my look. She just kept reading. Maybe I imagined her half-hearted, whiny plea.

I started to walk away, and she said, "Come on, Finn. Have a heart. I'm hungry."

"Mary?"

"I can be, if that's who you're looking for."

"What the hell have you done?"

"Sit down for a minute. You still angry with me?"

"I'm not the one who stormed out of the room last night."

"Yeah, I screwed up. I was so pissed off at myself for getting snatched by those three bastards that I took it out on you. It all went downhill from there. I felt like you were getting all possessive, and Mike was dismissive of my... Well, anyway I'm sorry. Think there's a chance I can recover?"

"I'm not sure, Mary."

She wiped a tear from her cheek with a grimy hand. "Please, Finn. You know how much you mean to me."

"No, I don't, really. But anyway, I'm not your biggest problem. You know where you stand with me. That hasn't changed. Missing that conference call this morning is a whole different thing, though."

"My phone kinda got broken." She rummaged in her backpack and brought out the remains of her custom, Phorcys-issued iPhone. Its screen was shattered, and the shiny metal case was bent at a sharp angle. "I was going to come by the room for the call, but I needed to be sure nobody was following me. I got into a little trouble last night."

"Were you serious about being hungry?"

"I could use a little breakfast, yeah."

"I was on my way to the marina to get a look at what's going on with *Anastasia*. This late in the morning, we might get a seat in that restaurant that overlooks the docks."

"Let's go, then." She stood up and swung the backpack over her shoulder.

I got to my feet and fell in step alongside her. "Did you smash the phone to cover yourself?"

"You think I would do something like that?"

"No comment," I said.

"I didn't. It was in my hip pocket when I got thrown down a ladder. I've got a matching bruise on my ass to prove it. Guess I need to tell you what happened, huh?"

"I'm not sure you should. Aaron's pretty good at reading me, after all the time we spent together."

"What are you trying to say, Finn?"

"I'm pretty sure I know what you did last night. What I don't know is why, or exactly how. And so far, it's all just speculation on my part. It might be better to keep it that way, assuming you're going to try to square this with our friends at Phorcys."

She walked along with a frown on her face, not saying anything for several seconds. "Yeah... I get what you're saying. If there's only one version of the story, they'll be more likely to accept it. Right?"

"Something like that, yes."

"But they know about us — our relationship. You think they'll believe I haven't told you what happened?"

"I've set the stage. When they asked where you were this morning, I told them you left last night to deal with personal stuff. I said that given our backgrounds, we didn't pry into each other's business. I figured that would keep them from asking too many questions."

"Thanks for that," she said. "Did it work?"

"So far, yes. I should tell you about the conference call. And before we get to the marina area, don't forget that Aaron has a surveillance team there. They're watching *Anastasia* and reporting back to him as things unfold. There are at least two people. A woman named Josie is in charge, and there's a man named Greg. I have no idea what they look like or where they are, and there may be more people I don't know about."

"Did they say anything about what happened last night?"

"No. Just about the marina manager finding the bodies this morning. I guess they didn't see anything remarkable during the night. They were watching the cops this morning. That seemed to be the first sign that something was wrong."

She nodded. "Should we go somewhere else, then?"

"Before we have any serious discussions, we should. I need to get a look at the situation there, though. Just be careful what you say, if anybody's in earshot. I don't know if the team will recognize me; they won't have a clue about you — not with your new look, that's for sure. Anyway, they're focused on the boat. They won't be watching the restaurants."

"You like my down-and-out college girl look?"

I wrinkled my nose and pinched it between my thumb and forefinger. "The look is only part of it."

She smiled. "That's all part of the disguise. I stole the clothes from a coin laundry. Unfortunately, they were still unwashed. I can't imagine what that girl did to make these clothes smell this way."

"Not sure I want to know," I said, as we climbed the steps to the door of the restaurant.

I was right about the place not being crowded. There was no hostess behind the podium; a placard invited us to seat ourselves. We found a table by the windows overlooking the docks. While Mary studied the menu, I took in the activity around *Anastasia*.

When the waitress appeared, Mary ordered a big breakfast; I settled for coffee. She excused herself to go to the ladies' room, and her food came as she slid back into the booth.

"Perfect timing," she said, sprinkling her eggs with salt and pepper. She stifled a yawn as she picked up her coffee.

"Sleepy?" I asked.

"Yes. I had a stressful night; couldn't sleep."

"I can imagine. I figured you got a room somewhere; I didn't expect you to stay out all night."

"I was too busy to bother with a room. Besides, I didn't want to miss you this morning. I thought you'd head this way once you heard the news."

"I didn't turn on the news. Did I miss something?"

"No. I meant the news from your phone call. My guess was they would still be watching *Anastasia*. But there must be something on TV by now, with all those news vans in the parking lot."

"Right," I said. "I haven't turned on the TV. When you've eaten, we should go back to the room and see what the story is."

"Do you think we can do that before I call in? And should I use a burner phone, or borrow your special iPhone?"

"That depends on how you plan to explain yourself, I guess. Think it over. If you use a burner, you can keep me out of it."

"You nervous about this?" she asked.

"No, not for my own sake. I don't have anything to hide; and I don't want you to tell me anything I can't share with Phorcys. But you need a coherent story about what you were up to while you and I were out of touch. There are some suspicious coincidences, from a timing standpoint. Just figure out how you want to play it and let me know."

She nodded and focused on finishing her breakfast while I watched the crime scene down on the dock. Two men were rolling a gurney with a bagged corpse down the gangway when Mary broke the silence.

"Okay. Here's the way I'd like to do this. You bought breakfast for a hungry girl who hustled you for spare change, if anybody asks. Maybe you figured she would be good cover in case anybody was watching for you. Don't mention meeting me, okay?"

I nodded.

"I'm going to leave you here," she said. "I'll use the women's showers at the marina to get cleaned up. By the time you see me again, I'll look like my normal self. While I'm doing that, you go back to the B&B.

"I'll call in from a burner phone and make my peace with Phorcys before I join you. You'll probably get a call from them telling you I'm okay and making my way back to you. By the time I get back to the room, maybe we can call in together and begin trying to make sense out of where we go from here. You okay with that?"

"Whatever you say; this one's all yours. I'm just along for the ride."

"Thanks, sailor."

"You're welcome, siren. Just don't lead me onto the rocks."

MARY LEFT, and I lingered over my coffee for a few minutes. When I finished the cup and waved off the waitress's offer of more, I picked up the check and took it to the cash register. Walking back to the B&B, I tried to imagine what kind of tale Mary would tell Phorcys.

From experience, I knew how creative and convincing she could be. As she put it one time, lying was a survival skill for her. In our early days together, we went through a few rough patches as we struggled with what the shrinks call "trust issues." Given our backgrounds, neither of us was inclined to be open about our activities when we were apart.

Mary and I worked as a team for the past few months, and we both thought our differences were behind us. Now, though, we were caught in a purely personal conflict. My attitudes and behavior were shaped by my career in the military; Mary didn't have that background. Our fundamental values and goals weren't in conflict. We resolved that question much earlier. We were at odds not over strategic direction now, but over tactics.

Mary wasn't accustomed to sharing the responsibility for operational decisions; she worked alone and followed her instincts. I wasn't bothered by that, but Mike Killington and Bob Lawson might be. Both of them were retired Army officers; they expected people to follow orders and stick to plans.

I crawled out of the same evolutionary swamp that they came from; I understood and trusted them. The same was true of Aaron Sanchez. I could no more lie to these men than I could jump over the moon; they knew me too well. They would see right through any deception on my part.

Mary's venture last night was the second time in a couple of weeks she had gone "off the reservation," as Aaron had put it several days ago. The first time, she had prevailed upon Bob Lawson to smooth things over. Bob brought Mary into Phorcys. He was not only her sponsor; he was her long-lost uncle. While that might bias a normal person, I didn't think for a minute that Bob would let a blood relationship influence his judgment.

From what I knew of their relationship, Bob tried to protect Mary as far back as her early childhood, but with little success. Still, Bob was a soldier's soldier. I had doubts about whether Mary could recover from this second transgression.

That worried me. I was committed to Phorcys and what it stood for; our country was in serious trouble. Phorcys was committed to our survival as a nation of laws.

I was also committed to Mary. Our mutual bond was stronger than anything I had ever known. Was it stronger than my commitment to the country I was sworn to serve?

I didn't know, and that was troubling. I wouldn't be surprised if Mary spun a yarn that convinced Bob Lawson and his partners that she acted in their best interests last night. I knew how persuasive she could be. But from my perspective, she indulged in a fit of pique when she took out Lavrov's crew on *Anastasia*. She was making her own rules, and I was afraid she might have blown our opportunity to learn more about Lavrov's operation.

Still lost in thought, I was surprised to find I was approaching the B&B. I went to my room, resolved to suspend making any judgments until I heard more from Mary and Phorcys.

24

I WAS STRETCHED OUT ON THE BED, MY FINGERS LACED BEHIND MY head, staring at the ceiling. Despite my determination not to make judgments without more information, I was getting worried. I kept glancing at the clock, wondering what was going on between Mary and Phorcys. Over an hour passed before my encrypted phone rang. I snatched it off the nightstand and hit the button to accept the call.

"Aaron?"

"No, it's Mike. Are you where you can talk for a few minutes?"

I rolled to a sitting position on the side of the bed, on full alert.

"Yes, sir."

Mike chuckled. "I know old habits die hard, but ease up on the 'sir' stuff. I haven't worn a uniform in a long time, and neither have you."

"Sorry, Mike." I fought to keep the anxiety from my voice.

"That's all right. Now, are you in a place where we can talk for a few minutes?"

"Sure. I'm alone in my room. What's the matter?"

"Everything's okay, Finn. Things are falling into place. We've heard from Mary; she's all right. That's the first thing."

"That's good. I've been worried about her."

"I imagine so. Now take a deep breath and relax. She's fine, and she's worried about how you will react to what she did."

"What she did?"

"Come on, Finn. I know Aaron told you about *Anastasia*. It doesn't take a genius to pin that on Mary. Not after what she did to O'Hanlon's bunch down in Martinique."

"Was she acting on your orders? For Phorcys, I mean? Was that sanctioned?"

"We'll get to all that. The answers to those questions aren't as cut and dried as you and I might like."

"I don't understand, Mike."

"Bear with me. You and I, we see things the same way. Good, bad, black, white. Salute and do your duty. It's the way we were raised; the way we were taught. Bob Lawson, too. It's ingrained in us. You with me?"

"So far, yes."

"Good. Bob and I and the others put Phorcys together because our way of protecting what we believe in wasn't working so well. There are a lot of reasons that's so. I won't go into all of them; there's one that's relevant to our current situation."

"What's that?"

"It's tough to articulate, so feel free to ask questions. The simple version is that we were playing by a set of rules that were out of date. The changes in our society have been increasing at an exponential rate for quite a while. The checks and balances we've depended on were put in place a long time ago. The opportunity for the corruption that plagues our government today didn't exist when our nation was founded. That's in part because of the pace of technological change, and in part because of the dramatic increase in population. Things happen faster than we can analyze them and react, nowadays. Are you still with me?"

"I think so, yes."

"Good. As we were developing the concepts that led to Phorcys, several people made the point that we needed new blood; all of us were cut from the same cloth."

"You're saying you needed people who didn't play by the same rules we all grew up with in the military?"

"Yes, exactly. We've all heard the clichés. 'It takes one to know one,' or, 'It takes a thief to catch a thief,' right?"

"Right. There's a lot of truth in those."

"Yes, there is. Clichés and stereotypes exist because at some level, they're dead accurate. We're dealing with a new kind of corruption, a different class of crooks, if you will. We struggled with how to staff an organization to deal with today's problems. Finally, we realized we needed people who grew up in the world that spawned the bad actors."

"That makes sense."

"Yes, it does. I thought you would agree, and I'm glad you do. Now I will move in a little closer to home, if you're still with me."

"Okay, I think I am. Give it a try."

"You know that we sent Mary to connect with you in Puerto Real when you were about to tackle Willi Dimitrovsky, don't you?"

I said nothing, letting the silence hang.

"It's okay, Finn. We know she told you, eventually. That was with our blessing."

"Okay. Yes, she told me. But only after I became part of Phorcys."

Mike chuckled. "Right. Buckle your seat belt; we're going for a wild ride. You ready?"

"I guess."

"Stop me anytime you have a question, okay?"

"Okay."

"Before we sent Mary to watch over you, we already expected that you would join us, eventually. We saw what was happening with your old group. Bob and I both kept a close watch on that. After all, it was our baby, all those years ago. We didn't doubt for a minute that you were going to join us; it was only a question of timing."

"Timing?"

"Yes. Once you figured out what they had become, we knew you'd part ways with them. We didn't foresee the details, but the end point was never in question — not for us."

"Okay. So why did you send Mary to look out for me?"

Mike laughed again. "I told you why on that first phone call with Aaron and Mary — the one where you figured out who I was, remember?"

"I remember the call, but I don't remember your telling me why you sent Mary."

"Oh, I didn't come right out and say it. But I did tell you that Bob Lawson said you were the most outstanding junior officer who ever served under him."

"I remember that; it gave me a serious ego boost."

"And it should have. Well, I just told you we both kept up with the goings-on in your old organization. We saw that you lived up to the promise that Bob saw 20-odd years ago. You're the best at what you do."

"Thanks, but I still don't see why you sent Mary to cover my ass."

"We had to tell her something to explain why we wanted her to shadow you. You know how she is; we needed a story that wouldn't set her off."

"I'm confused."

"It'll come clear soon. Stay with me, okay?"

"Sure."

"Mary figured out who Bob was about the time we told you about Phorcys. Until then, she didn't know he was with us. She shared their connection with you, didn't she?"

"You mean about his being her uncle?"

"Yes. He watched over her from a distance for years, after she rejected his offer of help. She didn't know that, of course. But he saw what she was becoming, and he saw the chance to help her grow in the right direction. At the same time, he thought she would bring an insider's grasp of contemporary criminality to our group. She's the first one of us who didn't come from a military background. We eased her into the operation. Started out contracting with her through her broker, until we got comfortable with her, and she with us."

Mike paused, and I said, "After you opened up with us on that phone call, she put all that together, more or less. And eventually shared it with me. But I still don't see why you sent her to cover me on the Dimitrovsky hit."

"Right. Now that you've got the background, I'll tell you. But I'll leave it to your judgment whether you should share it with her."

"Okay," I said, scratching my head.

"Her assignment was a combination of a training mission and a final exam, if you will."

"For which of us?"

"Come on, Finn. Now you're playing with me. For Mary, of course. We wanted her to see how an old pro did the job. And to see if she could keep up with you."

"I guess we both passed."

"With flying colors. And before I forget, I have a message for you from Bob."

"What's that?"

"You have his blessing. He's pleased with the way things have worked out between you and Mary on a personal level. And he said to tell you there's no pressure there. He knows how those things go. But he hopes it works out right for both of you, long term."

"Thank him for me."

"I'll do that. Questions?"

"Yes," I said. "About what Mary was up to last night?"

"That's what I've been leading up to. Mary doesn't see things the same way the rest of us do; that's why we brought her on board. She also thrived as a loner in her field; she's accustomed to making her own decisions. You may know that better than I do."

"Well, I won't argue with you about that. She's a poster child for 'Don't ask for permission, and don't even beg forgiveness unless they catch you.'"

That got a chuckle from Mike. "That's her, all right. She was badly shaken by being snatched off the street yesterday, and she was embarrassed that you rescued her. Right or wrong, she thinks she could have handled those two men without your help."

"Sensitive person that I am, I picked up on that."

"I'll bet you did." Mike laughed. "And she felt a strong need to kick ass. She was out to get even. Plus she was the one who was still exposed. 'For those old bastards behind the lines, it was all like an academic exercise,' she said to Bob a little while ago. 'I was the one with the target on my back.' What's your reaction to that, Finn?"

"I'm hurt that she lumped me in with the old bastards."

Mike laughed again. "I like you, Finn. I've admired and respected you for your accomplishments, but I didn't have a feel for what you were like, personally. That sense of humor is as much an asset to us as your skills. Now, what do you think of Mary's fear?"

"She's not wrong. She was the one with her ass in the line of fire."

"Yes. And by her reckoning, she has an absolute right to defend herself, even if we old bastards might prefer that she hunker down for a while. She was feeling threatened, and she acted to reduce the threat. Her only regret is that she missed Lavrov and his bodyguard."

"How do you and Bob feel about what she did?"

"We're coping with it. It's something we will have to deal with, if we want people with different perspectives to work with us. We're trying to keep our focus on the goal, not on the path. There are different ways to get from here to there. That's why we brought her in. It was inevitable that this sort of conflict would happen."

"What's your take on Mary?" I asked. "Do you and Bob think her independence is a threat to Phorcys?"

"No. Bob and Mary talked about that, and he and I discussed it before we decided to bring her on board. She's not confused about right and wrong — not one of those 'end-justifies-the-means' hotshots. He talked it over with her again, just now.

"We expected problems like this to happen, eventually. That strong independent streak coupled with her initiative made it inevitable. She's a keeper. The rest of us need to learn to deal with her and keep an open mind. There's a lot we can learn from somebody like that. She knows how the bad guys think; she's been there."

"So she's still with us?"

"Absolutely. Any other questions?"

"What happens next?"

"Before we move on to that, I need to tell you that Mary and Bob know that I was going to have this conversation with you. Beyond that, what we've talked about is just between you and me. I trust your judgment if you feel you need to share parts of it with Mary, but that's entirely up to you. And I agree with Bob about your personal relationship with her. We're comfortable that you're both professionals. What you do on your own time is between the two of you. We're happy for you if it works out, but there's no pressure either way. Clear?"

"Yes, sir. Sorry, I mean yes, Mike."

"That's okay," Mike said with a chuckle. "Now, what happens next is that Mary will get a text telling her I have briefed you. She's stuck with a burner phone; her encrypted phone was broken in the scuffle last night. If I don't miss my guess, you'll hear from her pretty damn quick. She's supposed to link up with you and the two of you should call in on your phone. Aaron will pass along our latest intel, and you can take it from there."

"Thanks, Mike. Nice talking with you."

"Same here. Stay well and tell Mary hello."

"Will do."

25

AFTER I TALKED WITH MIKE, I STARTED A POT OF COFFEE AT THE minibar to give me something to do. Before it finished brewing, the room phone rang. I picked up on the second ring.

"Hello?"

"Can I come up?"

"Yes, of course. What kind of question is that?"

"I wanted to be sure it was okay."

"Hurry up. Where are you?"

"The lobby. Bye."

Two minutes later, there was a soft tap on the door. I took the chain off and opened it. Mary stood there, looking nothing like the girl who ate breakfast with me two hours ago. She licked her lips and frowned.

"Can I come in?"

"What's the matter with you?" I swung the door open and motioned for her to enter. When I closed the door behind her, she licked her lips again, looking around the room like she never saw it before.

"Mary?"

She flinched and looked at me. "I'm really sorry, Finn. I want to explain, okay? I need your forgiveness."

"Everything's all right, Mary."

She shook her head. "No. I messed up; I need to — "

"You need to give me a hug, and then we need to call Aaron. Let's get the business out of the way first."

She dropped her backpack and stepped into my arms. Her head on my chest, she sobbed softly as I held her.

"It's all going to be okay," I said, patting her back.

"Oh, Finn, I was so scared I'd never see you again."

"That's all behind us now. Sit down and let me pour us coffee. We need to call Aaron, and then we can talk about us if you need to. But I'm just glad you're back safe and sound."

She straightened her back and nodded. With my arm around her, I led her to the little round table in the corner. She pulled out a chair and sat. Taking a step over to the minibar, I poured two cups of coffee and joined her.

"What did they... Who... Mike?"

"Mike called, yes."

"What did he tell you?"

"That you were safe, and that we're still a team as far as Phorcys is concerned."

She sighed, the hard angles around her mouth softening as she relaxed. "What did he tell you about last night?"

"Nothing, really. Not about what happened. Just that they were okay with it."

Her eyebrows rose. "That's all?"

I nodded.

"Then I should take a few minutes and — "

"Later, okay? Mike's instructions were for the two of us to call Aaron and pick up on the latest intelligence. Once we have that out of the way, you can tell me as much as you need to about last night. I'm afraid digesting your story might distract me from whatever Aaron has to say. All right?"

"But what if Aaron wants to discuss what happened?"

"Then we'll play it straight. But my bet is Aaron doesn't know any more about what you did last night than I do. And he's not going to ask. Trust me on that."

"I will, then. Bob told me the same thing. You guys all..." she shook her head.

"Yes, we do. We all think alike. That's why you're here, to give us a different perspective. Okay?"

"Okay. Make the call."

I took the phone from my pocket and put it between us on the table. I tapped in the unlock code and placed the call.

"Finn?"

"Yes."

"Mary with you?"

"I'm here," she said.

"Good to hear your voice. We missed you earlier. Did Finn fill you in?"

I nodded, and Mary said, "Sure."

"What's new from your end?" I asked.

"Greg tracked down the car rental information. It was rented to Nikolai Popovich. Florida driver's license, looks like a false identity. He's the bodyguard. There's nothing on Lavrov, or whoever he really is. We've run facial recognition on the driver's license photo. It's a match for a Russian national who is suspected of being part of an international criminal enterprise. He's the ex-*Spetsnaz* trooper, maybe. But his identity is fuzzy. He's used a lot of different names, and all the information in the files is 'rumored, unverified.' Anyway, he picked up the car late yesterday afternoon. He and the one calling himself Lavrov are unaccounted for, but they left the car at a self-service drop-off at the airport in Savannah two hours ago."

"So he and Lavrov are in the wind," I said.

"Yeah, but there's more. They may or may not be involved, but

Jeremy Theroux's body was found in his office first thing this morning. *Zamochit.*"

"Wait a second," Mary said.

"Okay," Aaron said, "What's up?"

"You guys didn't send that text we talked about, did you? The one to Lavrov, from Davies's phone?"

"No," Aaron said. "We talked about it, but there were a couple of things that held us up."

"I guess I was one," she said, "but what was the other?"

"I couldn't find the phone," I said. "I figured you must have ended up with it, somehow."

Mary frowned, looking at me.

"You were fiddling with it when we were in the car after we questioned him."

"I was?" She shook her head. "I'm still drawing a blank on a lot of that time. Wonder what they shot me up with?"

"Doesn't matter now," I said. "When I couldn't find it here or in the car, I thought maybe you dropped it in your bag."

She got up and retrieved her backpack, upending it, dumping its contents on the bed. After a few seconds, she held it up and waved it back and forth. "Guess it won't do us any good, now."

"It might," Aaron said. "You never know. Hang on to it until I get somebody to pick it up; we'll see where it leads. But let's get back to your question about the text. We didn't send it. We had reservations about it. I wanted to run some checks on the phone before we sent it, but we didn't have the phone — or the number. Plus, we wanted to find you first."

"Huh," Mary said. "I just wondered. So Lavrov must have had another reason for killing Theroux, then."

"Could be that he figured we were going to kill Theroux anyway, after we staked him out," I said. "And Lavrov wouldn't have wanted to take a chance on Theroux spilling his guts if we interrogated him."

"That would mean the Savannah target is in danger, too," Mary said.

"Yeah," Aaron said. "I was coming to that."

"Stringfellow is dead too?" I asked.

"Missing, so far," Aaron said. "Their housekeeper went to work this morning and found his wife all doped up and disoriented. Nobody has seen Stringfellow since he and his wife went to bed last night."

"Stringfellow is the guy in Savannah?" Mary asked.

"Right," Aaron said.

"My hat is off to you, Mary," I said. "You called Lavrov's move perfectly."

She gave me a searching look, then said, "You think he anticipated my text?"

I chuckled. "No, not that perfectly. But if we had sent it, he would have done your bidding, for sure. You didn't get to push his buttons, but you knew right where they were, and what would happen if you pushed them. I'm impressed."

"I think you're reading more into this than you should, but I appreciate the vote of confidence. I was guessing if I suggested it, he would kill them — kind of a macho thing. No way he would let a *woman* kill them. But the big question now is where do we go from here?"

"Mike and Bob called me a little while ago," Aaron said. "The consensus is that we need to let things cool off. Remember that DoJ investigation? I mentioned it way back, when you hit the Senator."

"The investigation into the mysterious Russian, you mean?" I asked.

"Yes. There were several other people under surveillance in connection with that, and all of them have died in the last couple of weeks, thanks to the two of you, mostly."

"Is somebody onto us?" Mary asked.

"There's no sign of that in our intercepts from the DoJ. But

Mike and Bob and the others worry that Lavrov might not be the only one who goes underground. They suggested that maybe you should go sailing for a while — get out of the States and let the dust clear. Meanwhile, we need to find Lavrov, or whatever his name is. And we're keeping a close watch on the players at the DoJ; we already know there's something rotten there. We need to let things quiet down, or all the rats will scurry away before we can find them."

"So we're on vacation for a while?" I asked. "Is that the idea?"

"Yep. But before you go, put Davies's phone in a padded envelope and leave it at the front desk. I'll send a courier around this afternoon to pick it up and drop off a replacement for that broken phone of yours, Mary. You weren't leaving today, were you?"

"Not today. I've got a night's sleep to make up."

"Rest well, then. You two take care, and I'll keep you posted on things here."

"Thanks, Aaron," I said.

"And from me," Mary said, as I disconnected the call.

I took her hand in mine and looked her in the eye. "Do you need to talk?"

She nodded. "I screwed up, Finn."

"You keep saying that, but I'm not sure why."

"Why what?"

"Why you did what you did, or why you think you screwed up. You're not impulsive; you don't do things without a reason."

"There's a lot buried in those statements. And yeah, what I did last night might have been a screw-up, even though Bob said I did what I thought was right. He told me nobody was going to second guess me about that. Bob said something like what you said a few minutes ago — that I have a different perspective on things than the rest of you. Different doesn't mean wrong, he said. But he gave me pointers on what I could have done differently to keep myself safer and avoid the confusion and disruption." She paused and took a sip of coffee.

"That's interesting," I said. "So why do you say you screwed up?"

"Because I did. I let those bastards get the drop on me. I should have been watching my back."

"There's nothing I can say that will make you feel differently. I know. I've been there. We all have. Mull it over, analyze what you could have done differently. Figure out how they got inside your guard. But don't beat yourself up about it. It's over. You survived; they didn't. That makes you the winner."

"Because I was lucky enough to have you looking out for me. That's not good enough."

"Now you'll hurt my feelings."

"No, Finn! That's not how I — "

"I know it's not. Forgive me for trying to interject a little humor. I shouldn't have; I know how raw your feelings are right now. Mine too."

"It's okay. But I never depend on luck; that's why I feel like I messed up. If it weren't for luck..." She shook her head.

"I would have never met the woman I love, if it weren't for luck, Mary."

"That's sweet, Finn. But it's not the same."

"Luck is a part of life," I said. "Sometimes it works in your favor, and sometimes it doesn't. But it's always there, tipping the scales one way or the other. If you don't like that notion, think of it as the sum of all the things that are beyond your control that influence the outcome of your efforts."

"I'm trying. Bob told me something similar. He quoted a French philosopher from the early 1800s. 'Chance is perhaps the pseudonym of God, when he does not wish to sign his work.'

"He said I should ponder that, if I wanted to come to grips with the role luck plays in our affairs. Pretty deep, huh? Do they teach you stuff like that in the military?"

"Sort of, via the method of hard knocks. What else did Bob

have to say? You mentioned pointers on how you could have reduced the risk of what you did last night?"

"Yes. Aside from wanting to strike back, my take on the whole situation was that I was the one they were after. None of you wanted to let me deal with that in the way I thought was best. Like I told you, that really pissed me off. So I decided to handle it my way, and you all could suck it up, or not. I told Bob I was sorry if I didn't follow orders like the rest of you, but that's the way I am."

"And how did he react to that?" I asked.

"He said something like, 'Mary, you were in the best position to make a decision about how to proceed. The decision you made was yours to make. But you should have told Finn what you planned to do. I understand that you needed to go in alone; he would have understood that, too. But you gave up any opportunity for assistance, because nobody knew where you were.'

"I never thought about that, Finn. I'm not used to having help, or backup. I just thought you guys would tell me I couldn't do what I thought I needed to do. So yes, I did screw up last night. But I guess I got lucky. It all went the way I planned it."

I nodded and didn't say anything.

"Actually, I didn't really plan it, just between you and me. I went to the marina to get a first-hand look at *Anastasia*. As I was walking out toward the face dock, these two crewmen wearing polo shirts with *Anastasia* on them passed me going the other way. One of them gave me the eye, and that's how it all started. They bought me a few drinks at the bar in the marina and I fed them a line about looking for a crew position. They offered to show me the yacht. How could I turn that down?

"I knew what those two were thinking; they were obvious about it. But I know my way around jerks like that. So they slipped me aboard, and I took it from there. They were planning for an early departure this morning, so most of the crew were already asleep. They died in their beds.

"Once I worked my way up to the captain's quarters, I took time to ask him a few questions. He didn't know where Lavrov and his bodyguard were — just that they would meet up in Savannah this evening. And that's about it. I saw an opportunity and took it. One of those *carpe diem* things."

"Were you expecting to find Lavrov aboard?"

"No. The two guys who picked me up told me the owner was away. That was why they could get away with sneaking me aboard. But I decided that was okay. I knew we didn't want to kill Lavrov before we learned more about him. Mike said that, remember? On our conference call. But he also wanted to shake Lavrov up, throw him off balance. I figured killing his crew while he was away for the night might rattle his cage a little bit."

Rattle his cage? A little bit? You killed 12 people to rattle his cage?

"No kidding. It will be interesting to see what his next move is. But my bet is he will lie low for a while. That's okay with me. I could do with a little break. Aaron as good as told us Mike and Bob want us to go sailing for a while — get lost in the islands."

"We could pick up where we left off," Mary said. "But *Island Girl's* out of the water, right?"

"Yes. I can call the boatyard and schedule a launch, though. Not a big deal."

"How long will it take to put her back together? You stripped everything on deck and stored it in the cabin, didn't you?"

"Yes. It'll take a few days to get her shipshape."

"Do you mind going down and doing that by yourself?"

"No, but why?"

"Just some things I would like to take care of. A few days should do it, and then I can fly down. Could we meet in St. Thomas in a week?"

I swallowed my disappointment, wondering what she was plotting next. "Sure. If that's what you want."

"And can we leave there right away?"

"I'd like that," I said.

"Me, too, sailor. Can we go back to Isla de Aves and chill out for a while? Just the two of us, with nobody else for a hundred miles?"

"Sure," I said. "We can do that." *I hear a woman's voice, singing, singing, calling to me...*

The End

MAILING LIST

Thank you for reading *Sailors and Sirens*.

Sign up for my mailing list at http://eepurl.com/bKujyv for notice of new releases and special sales or giveaways. I'll email a link to you for a free download of my short story, The Lost Tourist Franchise, when you sign up. I promise not to use the list for anything else; I dislike spam as much as you do.

A NOTE TO THE READER

Thank you again for reading *Sailors and Sirens*, the fourth book in the new **J.R. Finn Sailing Mystery Series**. I hope you enjoyed it. If so, please leave a brief review on Amazon.

Reviews are of great benefit to independent authors like me; they help me more than you can imagine. They are a primary means to help new readers find my work. A few words from you can help others find the pleasure that I hope you found in this book, as well as keeping my spirits up as I work on the next one.

In September 2019, I published *Villains and Vixens*, the fifth novel in the **J.R. Finn Sailing Mystery** series. The first four books of this series are also available in audiobook. A list of all my books is on the last page; just click on a title or go to my website for more information.

I also write two other sailing-thriller series set in the Caribbean. If you enjoyed the adventures of Finn and Mary, you'll enjoy the **Bluewater Thrillers** and the **Connie Barrera Thrillers**.

The **Bluewater Thrillers** feature two young women, Dani

Berger and Liz Chirac. Dani and Liz sail a luxury charter yacht named *Vengeance*. They often find trouble, but they can take care of themselves.

The **Connie Barrera Thrillers** are a spin-off from the **Bluewater Thrillers**. Before Connie went to sea, she was a first-rate con artist. Dani and Liz met Connie in *Bluewater Ice*, and they taught her to sail. She liked it so much she bought a charter yacht of her own.

Dani and Liz also introduced her to Paul Russo, a retired Miami homicide detective. Paul signed on as her first mate and chef, but he ended up as her husband. Connie and Paul run a charter sailing yacht named *Diamantista*. Like Dani and Liz, they're often beset by problems unrelated to sailing.

The **Bluewater Thrillers** and the **Connie Barrera Thrillers** share many of the same characters. Phillip Davis and his wife Sandrine, Sharktooth, and Marie LaCroix often appear in both series, as do Connie, Paul, Dani, and Liz. Here's a link to the web page that lists those novels in order of publication: http://www.clrdougherty.com/p/bluewater-thrillers-and-connie-barrera.html

If you'd like to know when my next book is released, visit my author's page on Amazon at www.amazon.com/author/clrdougherty and click the "Follow" link or sign up for my mailing list at http://eepurl.com/bKujyv for information on sales and special promotions. I welcome email correspondence about books, boats and sailing. My address is clrd@clrdougherty.com. I enjoy hearing from people who read my books; I always answer email from readers. Thanks again for your support.

ABOUT THE AUTHOR

Welcome Aboard!

Charles Dougherty is a lifelong sailor; he's lived what he writes. He and his wife have spent over 30 years sailing together.

For 15 years, they lived aboard their boat full-time, cruising the East Coast and the Caribbean islands. They spent most of that time exploring the Eastern Caribbean.

Dougherty is well acquainted with the islands and their people. The characters and locations in his novels reflect his experience.

A storyteller before all else, Dougherty lets his characters speak for themselves. Pick up one of his thrillers and listen to the sound of adventure as you smell the salt air. Enjoy the views of distant horizons and meet some people you won't forget.

Dougherty's sailing fiction books include the **Bluewater Thrillers**, the **Connie Barrera Thrillers**, and the **J.R. Finn Sailing Mysteries**.

Dougherty's first novel was *Deception in Savannah*. While it's not about sailing, one of the main characters is Connie Barrera. He had so much fun with Connie that he built a sailing series around her.

Before writing Connie's series, he wrote the first three Bluewater Thrillers, about two young women running a charter yacht in the islands. In the fourth book, Connie shows up as their charter guest.

She stayed for the fifth Bluewater book. Then Connie demanded her own series.

The J.R. Finn books are his newest sailing series. The first Finn book, though it begins in Puerto Rico, starts with a real-life encounter that Dougherty had in St. Lucia. For more information about that, visit his website.

Dougherty's other fiction works are the *Redemption of Becky Jones*, a psycho-thriller, and *The Lost Tourist Franchise*, a short story about another of the characters from *Deception in Savannah*.

Dougherty has also written two non-fiction books. *Life's a Ditch* is the story of how he and his wife moved aboard their sailboat, Play Actor, and their adventures along the east coast of the U.S. *Dungda de Islan'* relates their experiences while cruising the Caribbean.

Charles Dougherty welcomes email correspondence with readers.

www.clrdougherty.com
clrd@clrdougherty.com

OTHER BOOKS BY C.L.R. DOUGHERTY

Bluewater Thrillers

Bluewater Killer

Bluewater Vengeance

Bluewater Voodoo

Bluewater Ice

Bluewater Betrayal

Bluewater Stalker

Bluewater Bullion

Bluewater Rendezvous

Bluewater Ganja

Bluewater Jailbird

Bluewater Drone

Bluewater Revolution

Bluewater Enigma

Bluewater Quest

Bluewater Target

Bluewater Blackmail

Bluewater Thrillers Boxed Set: Books 1-3

Connie Barrera Thrillers

From Deception to Betrayal - An Introduction to Connie Barrera

Love for Sail - A Connie Barrera Thriller

Sailor's Delight - A Connie Barrera Thriller

A Blast to Sail - A Connie Barrera Thriller

Storm Sail - A Connie Barrera Thriller

Running Under Sail - A Connie Barrera Thriller

Sails Job - A Connie Barrera Thriller

Under Full Sail - A Connie Barrera Thriller

An Easy Sail - A Connie Barrera Thriller

A Torn Sail - A Connie Barrera Thriller

A Righteous Sail - A Connie Barrera Thriller

Sailor Take Warning - A Connie Barrera Thriller

J.R. Finn Sailing Mysteries

Assassins and Liars

Avengers and Rogues

Vigilantes and Lovers

Sailors and Sirens

Villains and Vixens

Other Fiction

Deception in Savannah

The Redemption of Becky Jones

The Lost Tourist Franchise

Books for Sailors and Dreamers

Life's a Ditch

Dungda de Islan'

Audiobooks

Assassins and Liars

Avengers and Rogues

Vigilantes and Lovers

Sailors and Sirens

For more information please visit www.clrdougherty.com

Or visit www.amazon.com/author/clrdougherty

www.clrdougherty.com

clrd@clrdougherty.com

SAMPLE OF BLUEWATER KILLER

Read the first few chapters of *Bluewater Killer*, the first of the
Bluewater Thrillers.

PROLOGUE

THE SUN HAD JUST DIPPED BELOW THE HORIZON, AND THE SEA surface was lit by that lingering glow that fades to darkness so quickly in the tropics. The man on watch in the freighter's wheelhouse caught a glimpse of safety yellow among the waves a few hundred yards off the bow, and then darkness fell.

A strobe light caught his eye as the scrap of yellow faded from view. He called to one of the off-watch crewmen to go up to the bow as a lookout while he altered course slightly, wondering what they would find.

The helmsman throttled the big diesel down and disengaged the transmission, allowing the ship to coast as they approached the strobe. A few yards from the flashing light, he went to full power astern for a moment to stop them.

The man on the bow turned on a powerful handheld spotlight. The helmsman climbed down from the wheelhouse and joined him.

In the light's harsh beam, they could make out a person in a bright yellow life vest. The person appeared to be unconscious, rolling with the waves, head and arms moving loosely.

The waves blocked their view every few seconds. The sea was

rough, and the man who had been steering didn't think he could maneuver the ship well enough to retrieve the person.

He went back to the wheelhouse, to the little cabin where the captain was asleep, and woke him. The captain took the controls and put the ship close alongside the person.

When the ship's pilot ladder drew abreast of their target, a deck crewman hanging on the last rungs of the ladder snagged the life vest with a boat hook. The helmsman joined him on the ladder, and they brought the person aboard.

CHAPTER 1

HE DRIFTED INTO CONSCIOUSNESS, FIGHTING IT THE WHOLE WAY. The harsh light of the sun burned through his eyelids. He clamped them closed, in hopes that he would drift off again.

"Where am I?" he asked.

No one answered, but his instincts told him that it wasn't a good place. As he raised a hand to his throbbing head, he smelled the corrosive vapors of jackiron rum wafting from his shirt.

Have I been drinking? Not much of a drinker, but I feel hung over.

Moving his hand to the floor, he felt the surface beneath him — hard, lumpy, and damp. Cobblestones?

He forced his eyes open again, a little bit at a time. His surroundings rolled past in surreal swirls. His instincts were right. He was nowhere good, and nowhere familiar, either.

Sunlight beamed from a hole, high up in one of the walls. He turned his head, trying to look the other way, but instantly regretted the effects of the motion.

Retching, he rolled onto his side to avoid choking. As the waves of nausea receded, he took in the uneven stone floor stretching from his cheek to the iron bars comprising the wall opposite the one with the hole in it. Bars? I'm in a cell.

"Where am I?" he asked again, in a loud voice.

Still, no one answered.

Ignoring his body's protests, he forced himself to a sitting position. He paused, waiting for his surroundings to stop their circular motion.

Alone. Dead quiet, but...

In the distance, he could hear voices, raised in gospel song. There was a subtle but noticeable calypso undertone to the familiar music. As he registered the rhythm, the notion that he was in the islands formed in his mind.

I'm hung over and in jail, somewhere in the Caribbean. Church service. Thirsty. Hungry. His stomach growled.

He crawled over to the bars and pulled himself to a semi-erect position. His vision swirled again; he clung to the bars to keep from falling.

Careful about moving my head so fast. He looked out into a dim, rough-walled corridor, broken pieces of oyster shell visible in the construction. Definitely in the islands.

"Hello," he called. "Anybody there?"

He listened as the sound of his voice died in soft echoes. Still grasping the vertical bars of his cell door, he shook it to make a noise and get someone's attention. To his surprise, the door swung out into the corridor with a loud screech of rusty iron hinges.

He stumbled, shuffling to stay on his feet, as he followed the arc of the swinging door. He paused, hanging on the door to regain his equilibrium. After a few seconds, he released his grip on the door and moved a little way into the corridor, taking in the empty cells to either side of his.

"Hey!" he yelled, rewarded by an increase in the throbbing pressure behind his forehead.

No one answered. Leaning on the wall, he worked his way

down the corridor toward what appeared to be an exit. Reaching the end of the corridor, he peered through a narrow archway into a sort of waiting room.

It was dirty but neat, in that way unique to official spaces in small Caribbean countries. There was a bench along one wall. Along the opposite wall, there was a counter, with a window of scarred, yellowed Plexiglas, like the ticket booth at a defunct theater.

There was nobody behind the window. He stumbled out into the empty waiting room. Looking around for a moment, he blinked in confusion. A single door stood open, leading outside.

Still unsure of his footing, he shuffled out into the morning sunlight, expecting to encounter a policeman at any moment. He was a little worried about how he would explain his accidental freedom if anybody challenged him.

As he staggered out of the door, he looked up and back, over his shoulder. A signboard hanging above the portal bore the legend, "Police."

He recognized his surroundings, now. Bequia.

Bequia is a delightful little island just south of the main island of St. Vincent. The streets were deserted, and music poured forth from every house of worship.

Sunday, for sure.

His grasp of his situation increasing, he recalled that he was here on his sailboat. He made his way to the town dock, remembering as he walked with uncertain steps that he should find his dinghy tied up there. Better get back to the boat and get myself out of town. No telling what I've gotten myself into.

There were several rigid inflatable dinghies, one of them his, tied at the end of the dock. He had painted the name of the mother ship, Sea Serpent, in 3-inch-high letters on both sides when he bought it. The dinghy was locked to the dock with a heavy cable and a padlock.

He fumbled in his pockets. Empty. No keys, no money, either. Police probably have it unless somebody beat them to it.

Normally, he would only have been carrying a little local currency and his keys. He would have left everything else locked away aboard Sea Serpent.

He scrounged around the foot of the town dock, looking for something that he could use to liberate the dinghy. Picking up two almost-intact bricks, he carried them out to the end of the dock. He put one brick down on the dock and pulled on the cable holding the dinghy.

Gaining some slack, he twisted a kink into the cable, positioning the kink on top of the brick. After smashing the kinked cable repeatedly with the other brick for a few minutes, he succeeded in breaking the cable.

He dropped the bricks in the dinghy, climbed in, and fired up the outboard. His head was clearing now, thanks to the adrenalin and the activity, and he was aching with his need for water and food.

Looking out to the west, he spotted Sea Serpent, swinging to her anchor out near the harbor entrance. He brought the dinghy alongside her and shut off the outboard. He set the bricks up on the side deck.

The companionway was locked, as he had expected it to be, but a few quick blows with one of the bricks solved that problem. He dropped the bricks over the side.

At least nobody bothered the boat while I was ashore.

He went down the companionway ladder and rummaged in the refrigerator, finding a bottle of cold water. He swigged it down, feeling it soak into the dry tissues of his mouth and throat. He got a pot of coffee and a pan of scrambled eggs going on the galley stove.

His physical condition improving, he checked in the chart table to find that his wallet, passport, and ship's papers were where he always left them. He scanned the papers, discovering that he left St. George's, Grenada, on Wednesday, October 19, and had not yet cleared in with customs and immigration in St. Vincent and the Grenadines. A glance at the digital wristwatch hanging by its strap above the chart table confirmed that it was indeed Sunday morning, October 23.

According to the clearance documents from Grenada, he had been bound for Rodney Bay, St. Lucia. He probably spent Wednesday night at an out-of-the-way anchorage and got into Bequia the next night, most likely after Customs and Immigration had closed for the day. That would have been Thursday night, but now it was Sunday. He frowned.

Puzzling over the missing time made his headache worse, but he forced himself to think through his probable itinerary. He couldn't account for Thursday, Friday, or Saturday.

The papers from the chart table provided no record of his having cleared into Bequia, which he would normally have done the morning after an evening arrival.

Maybe I got here late last night. He shook his head, dismayed at the gap in his memory.

His eyes fell upon the ship's log, sitting on the tabletop in front of him. He opened it to the last entry; he had anchored in Petite Martinique late in the afternoon on October 19. There were no more recent entries in the log. He found that strange, as he was meticulous about records.

There was no official record of his arrival, unless he had lost his copy of the clearance paperwork. He checked his passport for an entry stamp, but there was none. He always asked the immigration officer in Bequia to stamp his passport, even though they didn't routinely do so. He liked clean records. His whole life, he had carried this legacy of parental control. All rules must be obeyed.

Since he wasn't carrying any identification, the police wouldn't have known who he was. They didn't even lock my cell; I couldn't have been in much trouble.

He wanted to know how he had come to spend the night in jail, but he had no idea how to find out without risking being re-incarcerated. Screw it. It doesn't matter. But I'd better get moving, just in case. St. Lucia here I come.

As he leaned down into the cockpit to start the diesel, he noticed splattered blood all around the drains. Did I catch a tuna?

He couldn't remember. Tuna often bled a lot. He shook his head. I always clean it up right away, so it doesn't stain the teak. Cleanliness and order were deeply ingrained in his psyche.

Puzzled, he grabbed the windlass control from the cockpit locker and went forward to raise the anchor. He noticed more bloodstains, all over the teak decking forward of the coach roof.

What happened? Looks like somebody butchered a hog. I don't land fish up here.

He shrugged off his confusion and raised the anchor, lashing it securely in its chocks, ready for sea. As Sea Serpent drifted toward the mouth of the harbor, he uncovered the mainsail and laid the jib out on the foredeck, ready to hoist.

Out of the lee of the land, the breeze began to fill in, and he raised both sails. While he clambered back to the cockpit, the breeze blew the bow off to port and the sails began to flog on the starboard tack. He sheeted them in for a close reach, heading for the west side of St. Vincent, and shut down the diesel.

As Sea Serpent worked her way out into the open water beyond the shelter of Bequia Head, the wind built to a steady 20 knots from the east. He trimmed the sails and set the wind-vane steering.

Gonna go below; get a quick shower. Late morning, no traffic to worry about. Everybody else left hours ago. He turned on the radar, set a two-mile guard band to warn him of other vessels coming too close, and went below deck.

CHAPTER 2

Stripping off his filthy clothes as he entered the head, he was taken aback to find feminine undergarments hung out to dry on the towel bar.

On the counter, he saw a woman's shower bag with a few typical toiletries in addition to a comb, a brush, a safety razor, and a toothbrush. Where did those come from?

Nobody else was aboard — at 40 feet overall, Sea Serpent didn't have anywhere for a stowaway to hide. The undergarments were dry, so he put them on the berth just forward of the head along with the shower bag and cleaned himself up.

Shaved, showered, and teeth brushed, he put on fresh shorts and a clean T-shirt. Feel human again.

About the time he finished, he sensed from the change in Sea Serpent's motion that she was in the open water of Bequia Channel. Back up in the cockpit, he did a quick 360-degree scan of the horizon.

No other vessels were in sight, and it was a beautiful, clear day. Sea Serpent rolled along at her seven-knot hull speed under perfect sailing conditions.

He climbed back down the companionway into the main

cabin and took a quick look around, trying to figure out where the woman's clothes came from. In one of the lockers above the starboard settee, he found an unfamiliar duffel bag.

He normally kept that storage space clear for use by the occasional guest, but he couldn't remember having any company. He put the duffel bag down on the settee to open it and noticed an Air France baggage tag on one of the handles.

The flight was from Charles de Gaulle to Antigua several months ago. Doesn't tell me much.

He unzipped the bag to find a typical sailor's stash: well-worn foul weather gear, a good, sharp rigging knife on a lanyard, a couple of pairs of clean cut-off jeans, one pair of clean but well-worn full-length jeans, half-a-dozen cheap, souvenir T-shirts, two string bikinis, and a pair of beat-up sea-boots stuffed with several pairs of rolled-up woolen socks. This woman was a seasoned sailor, not a tourist.

Feeling around the sides of the bag, he found a zippered pouch, which held a wallet, a French passport, and a dog-eared spiral notebook. He opened the passport and discovered that it belonged to Danielle Marie Berger.

Even in a typical passport mug shot, she was a looker, a little French pixie with short, curly blond hair and an impish smile. You're cute. Where'd you go, anyhow?

The wallet contained a crisp 100 euro note and a few hundred Eastern Caribbean dollars in used small-denomination bills. There were no credit cards, although there was an ATM card for a French bank.

He noticed a week-old ATM receipt from the RBTT bank in Bequia. That's how she got the cash down here. Did I leave her in Bequia?

A French driver's license in the clear plastic window of the wallet matched the passport. There were no photos of family or friends, and none of the other miscellaneous items that he carried in his own wallet. Danielle travels light.

Opening the spiral notebook revealed that it was about one-third filled with notes in a neat script. I can't read much French, so it's not too helpful, Danielle.

On the last page, he noticed the date, 20 October, underlined. Following that, he read, "Sea Serpent, Mike Reilly, Mayreau, SVG." He frowned. That's my boat, and my name.

Mayreau is a small island about five miles north of Petite Martinique. Mike often stopped there for a night or two between Grenada and Bequia.

Working backwards through the notebook, he found that Danielle had been crew on the British yacht, Rambling Gal, for almost a year. Several of the stamps in her passport also listed Rambling Gal.

Head hurts. The sails began to flutter, making a racket. Mike zipped up the sea bag, stowed it back in the locker, and scrambled topside to mind his ship.

VISIT my website read more about *Bluewater Killer* and the rest of the series.